"We have eleven months of this marriage to go."

As she spoke, Gwen remembered the terms of their marriage agreement—a business contract—all too clearly.

"I know," Brad replied.

Gwen turned to face him, trying to speak around the lump in her throat. "Everything was fine until we—until you—" She broke off, unable to explain all that had happened to her.

"Until I kissed you," Brad supplied flatly.

"I think it would be better if we remained just friends," Gwen said in a rush. It hurt to reject even the temporary intimacy he was offering, but she had to do it. In the end she would be alone. Brad's exit from her life was as guaranteed as the one-year contract they had signed.

"All right . . . friends," agreed Brad.

"Good," Gwen said lightly. "That's all we are or ever will be."

Brad studied her face thoughtfully for a moment, then smiled. "We'll see. . . ."

Caroline Jantz, a Canadian author living on the coast of British Columbia, describes herself as the jeans-and-T-shirt type, who might consider marriage should she find that elusive hero of hers. Caroline first started writing her own private love stories when she was fifteen—all with happy endings—but didn't pursue her dream of a full-time writing career until after her second year at university.

Separate Lives

Caroline Jantz

Harlequin Books

TORONTO • NEW YORK • LONDON
AMSTERDAM • PARIS • SYDNEY • HAMBURG
STOCKHOLM • ATHENS • TOKYO • MILAN

Original hardcover edition published in 1986
by Mills & Boon Limited

ISBN 0-373-02793-1

Harlequin Romance first edition October 1986

this first book is dedicated
To Mum (Marj Rogan)
with special love

and

To Anne Kocherkewych
with special thanks

CHAPTER ONE

BRADLEY Robilliard leaned a shoulder against the far wall of his office and stared down at the busy streets of downtown Vancouver eighteen floors below. His hands were in his pockets, his shirtsleeves rolled carelessly part way up his forearms. Dark blue pin-striped slacks sheathed his long legs and clung smoothly to lean hips. His tough, supple body looked relaxed and there was no sign of trouble on his strikingly handsome face, but inwardly his mind was seething. Always controlled, always detached, his voice showed none of this inner disturbance when he spoke.

'I've never known you to joke about a serious business matter before, Leo.'

'I'm not joking,' said the man sitting comfortably in a black leather chair on the other side of the desk.

Brad turned his blond head and subjected his uncle to a cold glance. 'I think you are.'

'Then why aren't you laughing?'

'I don't find your joke amusing.' Brad straightened and returned to the chair he had left moments before. Reaching for his cigarettes, he sank into the padded leather and leaned back to study his visitor's face. 'Let's cut out the nonsense, Leo,' he suggested, withdrawing a filtertip from the pack and placing it between his lips. 'I need five hundred thousand dollars fast and you're in a position to lend it to me. Now will you or won't you?'

'So can your grandfather lend it to you.'

Brad flicked his lighter shut and exhaled a thin stream of smoke before lifting his cool blue gaze to his uncle's. 'We'll leave my grandfather out of this conversation, thank you.'

'Gladly.'

'Well?'

Leo Bennett casually crossed one leg over the other. 'As you said, I'm in a position to lend you any sum of money you need. I didn't get that way by joking about my business deals. My offer stands, with no room for negotiation.'

For the first time since Leo arrived, Brad showed some of the pressure he was under. 'For God's sake, Leo, are you out of your mind? Marry a girl I don't know just so I can get a loan from you?' He became aware of the office receptionist entering the room and sent her an impatient glance, not even realising that she must have heard what he'd just said. 'Yes, Penny, what is it?'

'You asked me to bring in this report from Accounting the moment it was delivered,' she replied after a startled look at Leo.

'Right. Thank you.'

'Howard Krieger's called three times this morning, asking if you're ready to sign yet.'

'Next time hang up on him.'

She nodded and returned to her outer office, closing the door softly behind her.

'Pushy fellow, isn't he, this Krieger?' Leo remarked.

Brad shrugged indifferently, his feelings once more tightly leashed. 'He likes to play games. The man knows damn well I stand little chance of raising half a million dollars cash in one week.'

'On the contrary, you stand an excellent chance.'

'But not one I'm prepared to take.' Brad flipped open the file before him. 'Are you ready to talk seriously yet, Leo?'

His uncle smiled. 'You're a stubborn son-of-a-gun, aren't you?'

'This report has all the details of the situation. Do you want to take a look at it?'

'There's no need. Krieger's taken over a loan agreement you made years ago, your accountant has disappeared with the money meant to pay it off, and now Krieger has given you an ultimatum—pay him five hundred thousand dollars by next Monday or Robilliard Enterprises becomes his lock, stock and barrel.' Leo waved a negligent hand. 'That about sums it up, doesn't it?'

'It does,' Brad said grimly.

'So what choice have you got? I'm your last resort, and you know it. All I'm asking in return for the loan is that you marry this girl and stay married to her for one year.'

'Oh, is that all?' Brad let a touch of sarcasm edge his voice. 'Are you sure you don't want a pack of kids from me as well?'

His uncle gave a rich chuckle. 'No, Brad, don't worry. A marriage of convenience, that's all I want. Gwen is my god-daughter and she's suddenly found herself needing a large amount of money. She won't take it from me and since I'm determined to give it to her, this seems the best way.'

Brad reached out to butt his half-smoked cigarette, his face devoid of any expression. 'And what makes you think she'll agree to marry me?'

'Oh, she'll agree, all right. She needs that money very badly.'

'But not badly enough to take it from you.'

'She refuses to accept charity,' his uncle explained.

'Come off it, Leo,' said Brad, becoming annoyed. 'There's more to this harebrained idea of yours than you're telling me. Now just what the hell do you have up your sleeve?'

'Absolutely nothing,' Leo answered firmly. 'I'll loan you the money you need on condition that you marry Gwen, and I'll give you whatever sum required to persuade her to marry you. What could be simpler than that?'

'Bachelorhood,' Brad snapped.

His uncle frowned. 'My god-daughter aside, don't you want to settle down and start raising a family some day, Brad?'

'I'm not the marrying type. Or the father type. Work is all I'm interested in, and a little bit of play.' Brad pushed back his chair and uncoiled his six-foot length to stand looking down at the older man. He was perfectly calm as he spoke the words that would destroy Robilliard Enterprises. 'Let's forget the loan, Leo. I started this company once and I can start it again.'

Leo rose, too. 'And your employees? Krieger doesn't like you, and you've already said that he plans to fire all your people if he takes over this place.'

For an instant Brad hesitated, then, implacably, 'They'll find other jobs.'

'I'm not so sure. Times are tough and jobs not so easy to come by these days.'

Brad rounded his desk. 'I'll walk you to the door.'

'Damned stubborn,' said Leo with emphasis, but there was a glint of admiration in his eyes.

Brad opened his office door and halted abruptly on seeing the crowded reception area beyond. Almost his entire staff was present, somehow knowing that their jobs depended on his meeting with Leo Bennett, and when he appeared in the doorway with his uncle a deadly quiet descended on the large room. Brad studied the anxious faces turned towards him in frowning silence. There was Jack Higgins, who had a wife and five children to support. Penny Hartwell was saving to buy a house with her husband, Lydia Salinger was a single mother raising twins, Geoffrey Adams was getting married next month. Brad had a heavy workload, but he nevertheless was aware of what was happening among his small but elite group of employees. Losing the company would be a bad blow to him, but he could handle it. To many of these people, however, the effect could be devastating.

Tight-lipped, Brad pulled Leo back into his office and closed the door. The two men exchanged a long, steady look before Brad turned sharply away, cursing softly beneath his breath. Only a certain desperation had made him apply to his uncle for a loan in the first place, after two days of trying to raise the money by other means. If he refused to accept Leo's condition, there was one more alternative. The thought flashed across Brad's mind only to be savagely thrust aside. He would do anything rather than approach his grandfather, even to the extent of paying an unknown girl to marry him, if that was what it took to secure Leo's loan.

He faced his uncle again, his eyes a cold blue. 'A marriage of convenience, to last exactly one year, with no other strings attached. That's the condition, right?'

'Yes.'

The blue eyes narrowed suddenly. 'I wonder which is more urgent, Leo, my need for your loan or your god-daughter's need for a husband.'

Leo smiled faintly. 'If you're thinking of trying to bargain with me, forget it. Gwen doesn't need a husband, she needs money. By agreeing to marry you in exchange for a handsome payment, she'll get that money and think it's earned rather than a charity hand-out from me. And if you don't marry her, I'll find some other method of helping her.'

'I applaud her high morals,' said Brad, with a not very pleasant curl to his lip. 'She won't accept charity, but she will lower herself to marrying for money.'

'None of that from you!' snapped his uncle in a sharpened tone. 'You'll treat Gwen with respect and kindness or the loan agreement ends, do you understand?'

'You're blackmailing me, Leo,' Brad warned, soft danger in his voice, 'and somehow I don't think you want to push me quite that far. Am I right?'

The older man showed the barest flicker of annoyance and Brad knew his guess was correct. What was the sly devil up to? A permanent husband for his precious god-daughter? Did he hope his nephew would fall head over heels in love with her and end up supporting her for the rest of her life? If so, his plan was going to backfire. Brad would marry the girl, but first he'd make damn sure she signed an agreement to divorce him after one year and not lay claim to any of his money or possessions. He'd made the mistake once of placing his trust in a woman; he wasn't about to make it twice.

He walked over to his desk for a pen and notepad. 'I hope to hell this Gwen is capable of understanding the ground rules, one of them being that she keep out of my way. Where can I reach her?'

'Oh, I don't think you need worry about her bothering you,' Leo told him, strolling forward. 'Gwen's the shy, quiet sort, inclined to stay well in the background and not make waves. She won't give you any trouble at all.'

An unholy gleam of amusement in Leo's eyes accompanied this bland assurance, but Brad was checking his calendar and not looking at his uncle, so missed what undoubtedly would have given him a strong foreboding of things to come.

The early morning sun found its way through the kitchen window to shine on the thin figure standing by the wall phone. It brought a dull sheen to raven black hair and showed a flash of green in a pair of tired eyes. Moving back out of its brightness, Gwen Shaughnessy gathered her robe more closely about her and listened anxiously as the phone in Toronto continued to ring. Finally there was a click and then a familiar, dearly loved voice coming over the line.

'Hello?'

'Hello, Grandma, it's Gwen. How are you doing?'

'Gwen! What a nice surprise. I'm doing fine, dear, all things considered. How about you?'

'Oh, me, too. Doing fine, I mean.' Gwen felt tears sting her eyes and fought to keep her voice steady. 'How's Julia? You said in your last letter that they were releasing her from the hospital this week.'

'That they did. We brought her home yesterday, and it wasn't a minute before the little honey was into my knitting bag. She had the wool spread out all over the place! But it was worth the mess to see the happiness in her face, Gwen. Four months in the hospital among strangers, her daddy gone and her mummy paralysed, casts and bandages all over her body——'

'She must be pretty excited to be with you and Grandpa now,' said Gwen.

'Yes, despite those heavy leg braces she's wearing, poor little tyke. Oh, wait, Grandpa's bringing her into the kitchen now. Julia, do you want to say hello to Auntie Gwen?'

There was excited chatter in the background and Gwen's fingers tightened convulsively around the receiver. If only she could be there with them to hug and be hugged! She needed what remained of her family, she needed them so very much.

'Hi, Annigun,' said Julia's little voice. 'Where are you? I'm with Nana and Gramps. They're gonna get me a dog for Christmas.'

'I'm in Vancouver, honey, getting ready to go to school again. What kind of dog are they going to get you?'

'I wanna black one. A *big* black one. When are you comin' to see me?'

'I don't know, Julia. But you're going to keep getting better, aren't you?'

'Yeah, an' I'm gonna do my ther'py so I can walk all by myself again. Nana and Gramps are gonna help me. Gramps wants to talk to you, Annigun, 'kay?'

'Okay. 'Bye, Julia.' There was a noisy clatter as the phone was obviously dropped in the transfer.

'Gwen?'

'I'm still here, Grandpa.'

'Sorry about that. Julia's still a little awkward with her hands.'

Gwen curled the telephone cord around her finger. 'She sounds good.'

'Yes, she seems to be taking her situation in stride. Never mentions Bob, though. Or your mother and father.'

She closed her eyes briefly against the sudden pain. Four months since the accident and her feeling of loss was just as deep and wrenching as when she'd first heard the news. Her grandfather's concerned voice came through the dimness.

'Gwen, your letters say you're just fine, but is that the truth? You're all alone out there and——'

'I'm okay, Grandpa, really.' The last thing the elderly couple needed was to be worrying about her. They had enough of a burden with a four-year-old invalid on their hands and another granddaughter in hospital with a broken back. 'I get low every now and then, but I'll be back to classes next week besides keeping my evening job, so there'll be little enough time to sit and brood. I just called to say hello for a change instead of writing. One long-distance phone call won't make me broke.'

'Do you think you'll be able to afford the trip out for Christmas? It would do Naomi and Julia good to see you—do your grandmother and me good, too. And this first Christmas after the accident you shouldn't be alone.'

'I'll try, Grandpa. Meanwhile, you take care of yourselves. Did you get that last cheque I sent you?'

'Yes, we did, but I still think——'

'Now, Grandpa, we've been through this before,' Gwen interrupted. 'My tuition and textbooks are all paid for, I have a roof over my head, clothes to wear and food to eat. I don't need any more than that. The main thing is to start paying off those hospital bills.'

A heavy sigh acknowledged the truth of this statement, but her grandfather still voiced a protest. 'Gwen, you're twenty years old, far too young to be burdening yourself with those matters. You should be out having fun——'

'We've been through that, too. We're all in this together, remember? Besides, this is my final year at university and it's important that I make good grades, so I won't have time for a lot of socialising, anyway.' Gwen glanced at the wall clock in the kitchen. 'It's almost seven my time, so I'd better go or I'll be late for work. Say goodbye to Grandma and Julia for me, and hello to Naomi the next time you visit her in the hospital. I'll write soon . . .'

Gwen hung up and stood staring unseeingly out the kitchen window, painful memories surfacing in her mind. Her parents had owned a shoe store in a small town up in the Interior of British Columbia, where Gwen had grown up. Last January the store, hitting hard times, had gone out of business. Dispirited, her mother and father had packed up their possessions and driven across Canada by car to live with her father's parents in Toronto until they were back on their feet again. With them went Gwen's older sister and brother-in-law and their small daughter. Only Naomi and Julia had made it though. Fifteen miles short of their destination, her parents' vehicle had been involved in a multiple car crash. Gwen had just returned to the dormitory

following her last university exam when the call came
from her distraught grandfather. Stunned and shaken,
her dazed mind trying to deny the tragic news, she had
flown to Toronto, only to return a week later with her
life drastically changed. Her sister, though critically
injured, was expected to live, but would need a series of
expensive operations if she were to ever walk again. Her
niece had several broken bones and would be in
hospital for a couple of months. Troubled and
depressed by the loss of his store, her father had let his
life insurance policy lapse. Bob, her brother-in-law,
had never even got around to taking one out. Nor was
his small family covered by medical insurance.

Lost in a nightmare of grief and rapidly mounting
hospital bills, Gwen could see only one route open to
her. Once back in Vancouver she took up her regular
summer job as an office assistant in a large marketing
firm and found a second full-time evening job as a
waitress in a busy downtown coffee shop. She moved
into a cheap little bedsit, sold the used car she had
proudly bought two years previously out of her own
savings, discovered ways and means of cutting her
living costs. Knowing that her chances of landing a
better-paying job would increase with a degree in her
hand, she made preparations to attend her last year of
the five-year business programme at the University of
British Columbia, her tuition already taken care of by
the scholarship she had won upon her graduation from
high school.

Now it was September, four and a half months after
the accident. Gwen had sent most of her wages from
her two summer jobs to her grandparents, to be used
towards Naomi's and Julia's hospital bills. But more
money was needed. The elderly couple had only their
home and their pensions, and it would be a heavy strain
on them financially to care for Julia while her mother
was in hospital. There were also the operations that
Gwen's sister had needed, as well as full-time nursing
once she was home and later the extensive therapy
required to complete her recovery. And if in the end
Naomi, despite all the medical help, couldn't walk,

she'd need money to support herself and her daughter
for some time to come.

All this had been discussed between Gwen and her
grandparents during that first terrible week after the
tragedy. As one alternative, her grandparents had
talked about selling their house to raise money, but
Gwen had instantly rejected the idea. She told them
that if they could look after Naomi and Julia, then she
could be free to work at paying off all the bills. It was
the only logical solution, but if Bill and Emily
Shaughnessy were to see the shape their granddaughter
was in they would have changed their minds immediately.

For the last few months had taken their toll on
Gwen. Working from eight in the morning to four in
the afternoon at her office job, then at five starting her
shift at the coffee shop and often not getting home until
midnight or later, she had had little time for thoughts
about her own well-being. It was easier to don simple
wash-and-wear clothes, easier not to wear make-up,
faster to eat on the run, more and more important to
make as much money as she could before classes began.
Her slim, five-foot-five figure had become thin,
emphasising the delicate fragility of her fine bones. Her
small, heart-shaped face with its flawless rose-white
complexion looked pale and washed out, the dark
circles beneath her eyes standing out noticeably. The
raven-black of her hair had lost its silky sheen, the hair
itself always pulled back into a tight ponytail now
rather than being allowed to fall in its usual thick,
bluntly-cut curtain past her shoulders. Her eyes were
heavy-lidded from constant exhaustion, their deep,
emerald-green depths lifeless except for the shadows of
grief that flitted in and out of them like ghosts, hinting
at pain which time didn't seem to be healing. Gwen was
suffering, but she refused to admit it to herself. She had
people depending on her for support, not to mention
her own livelihood to look after, and there was no time
for tears.

'Hey, you goin' to stand there all day, girl?'

The voice, raspy and grating on the nerves, jarred

Gwen's thoughts back to the present. She shot an anxious look at the clock and saw that it was seven-fifteen. She was running late.

'I'm sorry, Mrs Talbot, I was thinking,' she said, trying to slip past the small, grey-haired woman.

'Thinkin' about payin' your rent, I hope,' her landlady snapped. 'You're eight days late!'

Gwen halted, apprehension showing in her green eyes. 'Oh, please, Mrs Talbot, I'll have the rent for you on Monday, I promise. My boss at the coffee shop has been out of town and he won't be back to sign the cheques until then——'

'I better have it Monday or out you go. I don't run no charity house here—not by a long shot, I don't!'

The woman shuffled across the kitchen in her dirty robe and slippers and started cursing out the ancient stove. Breathing a sigh of relief, Gwen dashed downstairs to her tiny room in the basement. With a speed born out of habit, she finished getting ready for work, pulling on brown slacks and a beige pullover sweater. Minutes later she was outside running for the bus, her destination one of the many office towers downtown.

'You're late,' the receptionist said with a teasing smile when she arrived, flushed and out of breath.

It was exactly eight o'clock. Gwen smiled back and walked quickly to her desk in Accounting to start work. She was in the middle of a complex financial statement when the supervisor transferred a call to her just after eleven-thirty.

'Good morning, Gwen speaking.'

'Gwen Shaughnessy?'

'Yes?' The voice was attractively male, with a certain husky quality to it, and, extremely sexy. Even through her headache Gwen could feel the touch of magnetism in it, and she firmly suppressed a slight stirring of interest.

'My name is Brad Robilliard. I have a special reason for seeing you as soon as possible. When are you free?'

'I—beg your pardon?' she asked in bewilderment.

A trace of impatience edged the cultured tones. 'I

need to see you today, Miss Shaughnessy, on a matter
of business. What time is convenient?'

'Are you sure you have the right person?' Gwen asked
cautiously. Who in the world was Brad Robilliard? The
name was not even remotely familiar to her.

'Quite sure. The business matter is of some
importance. It would be to your advantage to meet with
me quickly. Are you free for lunch?'

'Yes, I'm—I mean, no, not lunch.' Chances were he
was inviting her to be his guest, but she wasn't sure, and
she couldn't afford to buy her own meal. 'What about
just coffee? I can——'

'Fine. There's a small restaurant around the corner
from where you work. I'll meet you there in five minutes.'

He rang off and Gwen was left feeling a bit ruffled.
Rather the autocratic type, was Brad Robilliard. *And* in
a hurry. What business could he possibly have with her?
Gwen took her handbag from the bottom drawer of
her desk and headed for the lifts. The early morning
sunshine had been replaced with dark clouds, and as
she left the building rain started to fall. Just my luck,
Gwen thought irritably. No umbrella and no coat, One
would think she'd be used to Vancouver's sudden
changes in weather by now and come to work prepared.
She quickened her step.

The restaurant designated as the meeting place was
sparsely filled, the lunch crowd not having arrived yet.
Gwen hesitated beside the empty cashier's counter,
scanning the occupants uncertainly. How was she
supposed to know the man she was to meet? She gave a
little shrug and headed for a table by the window. He
was the one who had made the appointment; let him do
the approaching. She ordered a coffee from the waitress
and settled back to wait. And wait. And wait . . .

'Boy, what a hunk! Wouldn't I just *love* to have *him*
in my bed!'

Gwen glanced over her shoulder. The gushing
statement came from one of three young women seated
at a table behind her. They were all staring in the
direction of the restaurant entrance, and with mild
curiosity Gwen followed their rapt gaze. A man in his

early thirties was just starting across the room. One hand was tucked casually in the pocket of his slacks, holding back the side of his black overcoat to reveal the light grey business suit beneath. The other carried a briefcase and dripping umbrella. He was, without exaggeration, the most stunningly handsome man Gwen had ever seen. His face was tanned to a golden bronze, the features perfectly sculptured, compellingly masculine. Piercing blue eyes were set beneath straight brows, the coldness in them matching the unsmiling line of his mouth. Raindrops glistened on the dusty blond hair, smooth and simply cut in a style which no doubt made some women long to run their fingers through it. He was tall, at least six feet, and carried himself with the co-ordinated grace of a natural athlete. Self-assured, controlled, coolly aloof, he looked to be the kind of man who went after what he wanted with the cold, precise strategy of a stalking panther. The thought caused a chill of premonition to sweep through Gwen and she shivered involuntarily. Then reason took over and she shrugged the feeling off. Whoever the man's target was, it certainly wasn't her. She returned her restless attention to her cold cup of coffee. Brad Robilliard was late, and if he didn't show up soon he could just take his matter of business and——

'Miss Shaughnessy?'

Gwen looked up, startled, to find that the blond stranger had stopped at her table. Close up, he was even more devastating. 'What?' she asked blankly.

'You *are* Gwen Shaughnessy, aren't you?'

'Yes.'

'I'm Brad Robilliard.'

He slid into a chair opposite her. The waitress appeared with far more alacrity than she'd done for Gwen and he ordered a cup of coffee for himself, not speaking again until it had been placed before him. Then, with no expression on his face at all, he opened the conversation.

'Thank you for agreeing to meet with me, Miss Shaughnessy. I don't know if I mentioned this on the phone, but I have a business proposition to lay before you.'

CHAPTER TWO

'PARDON?' Gwen asked, puzzled.

'A proposition. A deal. A——'

'Thank you, I know what the word means. What kind of proposition?'

A cigarette appeared and was lit with an economy of motion, much to her annoyance. Restoring the lighter to his pocket, Brad Robilliard leaned back in his chair and flicked a disinterested glance over her, taking in the tight black ponytail and pale face, the lack of any sparkle in her eyes. Gwen cupped her forehead in her hands and closed her eyes as sudden weariness swamped her. She wanted to sleep so badly, wanted to have the time to look nice, wanted to wake up in the morning without feeling panicky about all the money she needed. She did *not* want men like the one across from her butting into her life with mysterious and probably unsavoury propositions and feeling free to give her insolent inspections that made her aware of how rotten she looked. She felt like telling him to take his handsome, well-tailored self elsewhere, but her tiresome conscience demanded that she be polite.

'What kind of proposition?' she asked again, trying to rub away her headache.

'I understand you need money.'

Slowly, not sure if she'd heard correctly, Gwen raised her head to stare at him. 'What?'

'It's not true?'

She straightened, suddenly wary. 'Who told you that, Mr Robilliard?'

'The person's name is of no importance.'

Gwen frowned. She'd been too busy this past summer to keep up friendships, and as a result few people knew about her difficulties. So where would this man have got his information? She said guardedly, 'Are you saying this proposition of yours has to to with money?'

He stubbed out his cigarette and sat forward, lowering his voice in order not to be overheard. 'If you will marry and live with me for one year I will give you twenty thousand dollars plus a monthly allowance of five thousand dollars, with a lump sum of seventy thousand dollars at the end of the twelve months, the marriage to be strictly platonic.'

'*What?*' squeaked Gwen. Strictly platonic! What woman could be strictly platonic with a man like him around the house? Heavens, what on earth was she thinking about that for? *Marriage?* 'Marriage?' she said aloud, her expression incredulous. '*That's* the proposition?' He was silent, studying her reaction, and she hastily gathered her startled thoughts together. 'You can't be serious!'

'I'm quite serious,' he said evenly. 'If I marry by next Monday I'll receive a great deal of money. Someone suggested you.'

'Someone suggested——' Suspicion dawned. '*Who* suggested me?' she demanded.

'Someone who knew you needed money, obviously. I wasn't told why, and I'm not particularly interested.'

No, he didn't look too interested. Cold-blooded, certainly. Arrogant, as well. Did he really expect her to take him up on his offer?

'Mr Robilliard, you're a complete stranger to me, and even if you are serious I wouldn't for one moment consider your proposition. If I ever decide to marry, it will be for love, not money, and even then not until I'm well into my career.'

'Miss Shaughnessy, I am totally indifferent to your reasons for refusing. A simple yes or no will suffice. However' his electric blue eyes drilled into hers, 'I would like you to listen to the rest of it before giving me your final answer.'

Gwen felt almost hypnotised by his gaze, and could only nod wordlessly. A glint of satisfaction was swiftly masked.

'If you agree to the marriage, you will share my apartment with me, have your own room with adjoining bath, plus unlimited use of the building's pool and other recreational facilities. We will each live separate lives, free to form outside relationships, but bound by contract to fulfil certain obligations.'

'Which are?' Gwen asked uncertainly.

He shrugged his broad shoulders. 'Very few. I'll pay the advance and allowance, the lump sum, all living expenses such as rent, food, utility bills, and so forth, and anything else that comes up as a result of your living with me. All you have to do is reside in my apartment for a full twelve months and spend your money on whatever you please. And marry me, of course,' he added with a touch of irony.

Gwen cleared her throat. 'And—um—would the arrangement have to be a secret?'

One eyebrow rose. 'Hardly. I have no intention of curtailing my activities to suit the situation, and as some of those activities include women I don't think it would be quite honest of me to hide you in the closet.'

Lucky women, Gwen thought enviously, and gave herself a mental kick for her uncharacteristic reaction. What in heaven's name had come over her? He was just a *man*, for pete's sake! Albeit a handsome man. A *gorgeous* man, she amended, stealing a covert glance at his hard, chiselled features. A question occurred to her and she voiced it, telling herself that she was only curious.

'And at the end of the twelve months? We'd—there'd be a divorce?'

'An annulment,' he corrected briefly. 'The marriage would be unconsummated, after all.'

For the life of her, Gwen couldn't prevent the fiery blush that rose to her cheeks. Damn, damn, damn! Now he was going to think her an innocent little virgin. Which was true, but her lack of experience was not something she cared to advertise. She darted a resentful look at him and surprised an unexpected gleam of humour in his eyes, as if he knew exactly what she was thinking. It was gone in a flash and his expression was once more detached, but for a moment there he had actually looked human. Gwen hesitated, then took the more sensible route.

'Mr Robilliard, I don't know you from Adam, and I'm not prepared to risk moving in with a strange man. I'm sure you——'

'Believe me, Miss Shaughnessy, your virtue is safe with me. I'm not in the habit of seducing innocent lambs like you.' His tone was bored, as if he'd been unnecessarily put to the trouble of stating an obvious fact.

Gwen, ever polite, bit off the nasty retort she'd been about to make. 'I'm sorry to disappoint you, Mr Robilliard, but again, the answer is no.'

'I'm not disappointed,' he said indifferently, standing up. 'Finding a woman willing to marry for money presents little difficulty. Thank you for your time, Miss Shaughnessy.'

He left the table with unhurried strides, leaving Gwen to look after him open-mouthed. She hadn't expected the discussion to end so abruptly, had in fact expected him to use a little persuasion. Not that she'd wanted him to raise the price. She would never have agreed to such a preposterous deal, no matter how much money she was offered. Besides, she didn't want to get married yet, even for convenience. After her graduation next spring, she intended to join one of the large, successful companies in Vancouver and start working her way up the corporate ladder. Marriage and children, with all the attendant distractions, did not fit into this scheme, and possibly never would Still, there was a faint feeling of regret that Brad Robilliard had gone. Something about him had attracted her ... not just his looks, but something indefinable. A sense of security, perhaps, as if he could take all her troubles and make them disappear. Which he certainly could if she took his money.

A frown briefly touched Gwen's forehead. And that was another thing. How did he know about her, about her desperate need? Was he perhaps some colleague of Bob's. Someone who had known her dead brother-in-law and was choosing this anonymous way to help his friend's widow and child? If that were so, she could understand his method. Heaven forbid that a tough, unfeeling man like Brad Robilliard show any hint of kindness or generosity. He probably thought it would ruin his hardheaded reputation.

Gwen's thoughts turned, as they so often did, to the needs of her family. And that was when she realised that she had just selfishly turned down an opportunity to help them. What did pride and independence mean when faced with the knowledge that Naomi was worried sick about the lack of money instead of concentrating on getting better? And that her elderly grandparents were left to cope with a lively four-year-old whose main purpose in life seemed to be to get into as much mischief as possible, regardless of the casts that hampered her movements? Gwen would willingly sacrifice anything, including her principles, if by doing so she could bring much-needed relief to her beloved family. Yet still she hesitated. If a large amount of money appeared suddenly, it would require some sort of explanation. What would her grandparents feel on knowing that a granddaughter of theirs had, to all intents and purposes, sold herself for a hundred and fifty thousand dollars? And Naomi. Gwen didn't have to wonder about that. Her sister would be furious, partly at Gwen, partly at herself for being unable to pay the debts that were so rapidly piling up.

Gwen grabbed her handbag and half-ran to the cashier's desk. There was no other solution to their dilemma. She was running herself into the ground and about ready to collapse. If that happened, they would all suffer. She would marry Brad, and never mind the consequences. Her family was all that mattered now.

'How much do I owe you?' she asked the cashier, digging in her wallet for change.

'The blond gentleman paid the bill, dear.'

'He did? Okay, thank you.'

Gwen hurried to the door. He hadn't been gone long. If she could just catch him before he disappeared into the crowds . . .

She stood out on the sidewalk, unheeding of the drenching rain as she looked desperately around for Brad Robilliard's retreating figure. Wait, was that him getting into a car? She noted the belted black topcoat, glimpsed blond hair beneath the sheltering umbrella, and with relief dashed from the sidewalk to stop him, in her blind haste completely forgetting to look for oncoming vehicles. The next thing she knew she was being hauled roughly against a hard male chest, a car was passing by with an angry blare of its horn, and her canvas handbag was on the ground being thoroughly soaked.

'You could have been killed, you know.'

Brad's voice was calm, but Gwen could feel the rapid rise and fall of his chest. He'd had to move fast to pull her to safety. She looked up into his face and her heart inexplicably stopped.

'Your handbag is getting wet,' he pointed out.

'What? Oh. Yes, it is.'

His arms dropped from around her and he stooped to pick it up. They were both standing by the open car door, the rain slashing down on their unprotected heads. Gwen accepted her bag from him and said hesitantly, her attention on the ruined material, 'If . . . if you offer's still open, I'd like to take you up on it.'

'It's still open. Come on, let's get out of this rain.'

She balked as he made to put her into his car. 'I'll get the seat covers wet.'

'So will I. They're not important. Now get in before we both drown.'

Gwen got in, awkwardly scrambling past the steering wheel and over the gear-lever to the passenger seat beyond. Brad slid in after her and slammed the door shut.

'Damned rain!' He raked long fingers through his wet hair before reaching into the back seat for his briefcase, careful to conceal his relief that she hadn't called his bluff. The thought of returning to her in a more humble frame of mind had been galling. 'There's an agreement I want you to sign before we marry. It's just the written form of what I told you in the restaurant.'

Gwen shivered. Her clothes were plastered to her body, water from her hair dripping steadily down her neck. Brad gave her an all-embracing look, his bright gaze resting briefly on the firm thrust of her breasts beneath the wet sweater, then he was shrugging out of his overcoat and draping it over her.

'Do you make a habit of walking around in the rain without a coat?' He handed her a freshly-laundered handkerchief. 'Here. Wring out your hair.'

'Thank you. You're very considerate.'

'I don't want you dying of pneumonia before we're married,' he said drily.

Lesson number one, Gwen told herself. It will be a paper marriage only. Don't expect him to feel any kind of liking for you.

'May I see the agreement?' she asked stiffly.

She read it thoroughly—it was short and to the point, but included a clause he hadn't told her about. She caught her breath indignantly. She didn't *want* to lay claim to any of his money or possessions after the year was up, thank you very much. Of all the arrogant . . .! Wordlessly, Gwen took the pen he held out and signed her name to the bottom of the page, resolving to show Brad just how little she meant to have to do with him.

'Why do you have to marry to get the money you want?' she asked, handing pen and paper back to him and feeling very much as if she had just signed away one year of freedom and independence.

'To get a loan from my uncle to save my company,' he replied tersely, and changed the subject. 'I'll need your full name as well as your date and place of birth in order to apply for the marriage licence. And your current address. We'll be married on Monday. What time is convenient?'

'Any time in the morning. I start my new term at university next week, but my first class isn't until two o'clock in the afternoon.' Gwen was surprised he'd asked. From the impression she'd gained of him, he was more inclined to give orders. 'Don't I have to have a blood test, too?'

'Blood tests are no longer required in this province. What's your phone number?'

'I don't——' She stopped, then gave him Mrs Talbot's number, as well as all the other information he needed.

'That's that, then.' Brad closed his briefcase and tossed it back into the rear seat. 'I'll drive you home now,' he said, starting the engine.

'No, it's all right. I can take a bus.' First, though, she'd phone the office and tell them she couldn't make it back for the afternoon, not in her wet clothes. She reached for the door handle, but the car was already moving.

'I doubt if any self-respecting driver would let a drowned rat like you on his nice dry bus,' Brad remarked sardonically.

Gwen realised that it would be useless to argue. Besides, she was tired and wet and in no condition right now to hold her own against this supremely confident, not entirely pleasant man. But if he thought she was a meek little mouse to be walked on he had another think coming, that was for sure!

They drove in silence to the area where she lived, Brad obviously having memorised the address he'd written down. Fortunately, the outside of the Talbot house showed no sign of the cheap lodgings within. The car came to a stop in the driveway and Gwen returned his coat and handkerchief to him before opening the door.

'I'll phone you tonight with the details,' he said curtly.

'Yes. Thanks for the ride. 'Bye!'

She ran to the basement door, fumbled with the lock, then was inside and heading for the room allotted to her. Grabbing a towel, she hurried upstairs to the kitchen phone and dialled the coffee shop where she worked evenings and weekends. 'Bernie, it's Gwen. Listen, I'm free early today. Do you need an extra waitress?' She rubbed at her wet hair with the towel, waiting for the assistant manager to get back to her. 'You do? Good. No, no, I'll work my regular shift as well. I could use the extra money, that's all. Okay, I'll be there in half an hour. Thanks, Bernie.'

Gwen was once more travelling at a speed too fast to keep up.

*   *   *

She returned home at two in the morning, having
stayed late at the coffee shop to work a few extra hours.
A note was taped haphazardly to her door, telling her
to phone Brad. With a sinking feeling she remembered
that he'd said he'd call her that evening. Knowing that
she'd probably wake him up, she nonetheless tiptoted
upstairs to call him right then and there. It was the only
time she would be free from her landlady's inquisitive
ear, and she wanted no one to overhear her end of the
conversation.

A sleepy, irritable voice answered the phone on the
sixth ring, and for a second Gwen wasn't sure if it was
him. 'Hello? Brad Robilliard?'

'Who is this?'

'It's Gwen—Gwen Shaughnessy. You—left a message
asking me to call.'

'Oh, hell, not in the middle of the night!'

'I'm sorry. I just came in, and this is my only
opportunity to talk privately.'

'Been out sowing your wild oats, have you? Where's
that damn light?'

Gwen heard a crash, followed by a muttered curse
from Brad. 'Are you all right?' she asked anxiously.

'Fine, thank you,' he said with cutting politeness.
'Okay, it's set for Monday morning at eight-thirty. The
marriage commissioner will perform the ceremony at
my apartment.' He gave her the address, which she had
to memorise for lack of pen and paper. 'We'll need two
witnesses. I've got a friend lined up. Do you want me to
get the other one, too?'

'No, I'll—I'll bring my own. How long will it take, do
you know?'

'Not long. I can't spare any more time than necessary
from my office. That's it. I'll see you Monday. Good
night.'

There was a click and he was gone. Gwen slowly set
the receiver back in its cradle, feeling strangely let
down. She had wanted to talk to Brad, hear his voice
again, perhaps only to feel reassured that she wasn't
marrying a total stranger. After all, they'd be living
together for one year, and it would be nice if they could

live as friends. But he *was* a stranger, and she realised with a pang that he always would be, that he had no desire to be anything else.

She went to bed and four hours later was up getting ready for her last day at the office. That evening she worked her usual shift at the coffee shop, and double shifts Saturday and Sunday, convincing herself that she was only making sure of some extra money. But what she was really doing was keeping herself too busy to worry about whether her coming marriage was right or wrong. Yet still she lost sleep over it, and when Monday morning came she had succeeded mostly in exhausting herself and putting her mind in chaos.

'Some bride you are,' Gwen told her reflection in the mirror, once she'd finished dressing. She was wearing a grey skirt, with a matching jacket over a loose white blouse. It wasn't her best outfit, but it disguised her thinness to some extent, and Gwen was hoping to avoid an explosive lecture from her best friend.

Her hope wasn't realised. The bus from Vancouver Island was just pulling into the depot when Gwen arrived, and Kelly James was the first one off. She hugged Gwen tightly, all her sympathy in that long embrace, then she stepped back to give vent to anger.

'Dammit, Gwen, you told me you were doing fine! Look at you—you're a walking skeleton!'

'I'm not that——'

'You are so.' The vibrant redhead dragged her over to an isolated corner. 'Sport, I can understand why you never wrote to me about your parents and sister. I was trekking around Europe and it was hard for a letter to catch up to me. But when I got back last week and phoned you at the number you'd left with my mother— Gwen, you said you were *fine*, that you were dealing with it. If I'd known you were in this shape I would have come over from Victoria right away.'

'Your classes were starting at university and I——'

'Dammit, Gwen, my classes mean nothing to me when you're in trouble! What's the matter?'

This as Gwen suddenly leaned against a steel pole. 'I'm just . . . I'm tired, that's all.'

'I'm not surprised, working two full-time jobs like you've been doing,' said Kelly severely. 'And what about this marriage business? You call me yesterday morning and tell me you're getting married today. No explanations, just a simple request to come over and be your witness.'

'You didn't have to come,' Gwen said in a low voice. 'If you were busy . . .'

'I'm here, aren't I? Sport, you haven't told me anything about the groom, not even his name!'

'His name's Brad Robilliard.'

'*What!*'

Gwen eyed her friend uneasily. The mention of Brad's name had turned Kelly to stone. 'I said——'

'I heard what you said! Of all the men in the world to pick!' Kelly took a deep breath and continued deliberately, 'Gwen, you will marry Brad Robilliard over my dead body.'

'I take it you know him,' Gwen ventured.

'*Know* him! He doesn't *let* anyone *know* him! But I've met him, and a more cold-hearted, cynical, self-centred——'

'K.J., he can't be all that. I mean, well . . .'

'He's all that and more! My oldest sister dated him for two months and from what she told me——'

'Kelly, you surely can't be basing your opinion on what Anita said of him?' Gwen broke in, hotly indignant. 'You know very well she slanders anyone she doesn't like, and if Brad only dated her for two months you can bet the break-up was his idea and she took it in bad part.'

'Are you saying that my sister is a liar?' the other girl demanded aggressively.

'You're the one who told me she is, and I've seen it for myself.'

There was a pause.

'Well, she is,' Kelly acknowledged grudgingly. She scowled. 'But that's beside the point. Do you *love* him, Gwen?' Her tone clearly indicated that she felt it impossible for any woman to love Brad.

Gwen fidgeted with her bag strap. 'I need a great deal of money, K.J.'

'You told me that on the phone. What with all the hospital bills and——' Kelly broke off, then, ominously, 'Gwendolyn Meredith Shaughnessy, are you telling me that you . . .'

A young couple passed by, giving the two girls curious looks. Kelly waited for them to get farther away before continuing. 'Are you marrying him for his *money*?' she hissed incredulously.

'He came to me last Thursday, offering a marriage of convenience,' Gwen told her. 'I get a total of one hundred and fifty thousand dollars if I stay married to him for one year.'

'I don't believe I'm hearing this! You, of all people!'

Gwen straightened. 'Please understand, Kelly. Naomi and my grandparents are so worried about those bills. It's costing over ten thousand dollars for each month that my sister is in the hospital. And my grandparents don't have it easy themselves. We need *money*, K.J., and if I can get it by marrying Brad Robilliard, then I will.'

All the anger went out of the redhead's face. 'I'm sorry, sport, I guess I didn't realise just how bad it was. I understand, honestly. But . . . Brad Robilliard?'

'I only met him briefly, K.J., but he seems all right. A little inhuman, that's all. And it won't be so bad. It'll be just like sharing an apartment with any other roommate, except that Brad will pay all the bills. I probably won't see much of him——'

'No, he'll be out chasing women, if his reputation is anything to go by. Why does he have to marry, anyway?'

'To save his company . . .'

'Typical of him! He certainly wouldn't marry for love.'

'. . . and because his uncle won't lend him the money to do so unless he does,' Gwen added.

'See? His own family is trying to get rid of him.'

'Kelly!' Gwen sighed in exasperation.

'Okay, okay, I said I understand your reasons for marrying him and I won't interfere. I just don't like the idea of Brad being your groom.'

Apprehension crept over Gwen as Kelly's words prodded the doubts she had deep down about the step she was about to take. She'd be living with a stranger, a man who had proved himself to be cold, indifferent, sardonic, unfriendly. Those were all negative signs, a warning that it might be unwise to allow herself even a limited involvement with him. He cared too little about people to let anything disturb his mental and emotional equilibrium. That was Gwen's impression of him, and she felt reassured by it. Partially. With false bravado, she gave her friend that same reassurance.

'Nothing's going to happen, K.J. It will be a strictly platonic relationship with, I'm sure, very little contact between us. He'll go his way and I'll go mine, and after one year we'll get an annulment. It's as simple as that.'

Kelly snorted, unbelieving. 'Somehow I don't think it's going to stay that simple.'

The argument over, they caught a bus to Brad's apartment, which turned out to be a suite in an exclusive, multi-levelled complex on Beach Avenue, overlooking English Bay. The door was opened by a dark-haired man dressed casually in corduroy slacks and a sports jacket. His gaze zeroed in appreciatively on Kelly before flicking to her pale companion.

'You must be Gwen. I'm Shane Michaels, a friend of Brad's. Come on in.' He stepped back to allow them to enter. 'Brad's on the phone right now—a crisis at the office. This way.'

Gwen and Kelly followed him down the two steps from the foyer and through an open area to the stairs leading down to a large, high-beamed living-room. Brad was standing at the portable bar in the corner, speaking with clipped words to the person on the other end of the phone. He shot a look in their direction and ended the conversation abruptly.

'Look, Corinne, I have to go. I'll be in the office by nine and we'll go over the problem then.'

He hung up and crossed the room to join them. Gwen's gaze flitted nervously over the dark brown three-piece suit which had obviously been tailor-made to fit Brad's tall, lithe body. More handsome than she remembered, he looked the picture of cool, sophisticated success, and Gwen had the fleeting thought that she could, with very little effort, find herself romantically interested in him. The idea alarmed her, and her body actually flinched, as if feeling ahead of time the hurt this man could inflict with one single word, one burning touch. Nonsense, she told herself, flustered. He's not your type and is far from being even likeable, so you couldn't possibly fall in love with him. The logic of that instilled confidence in her immunity to his blond good looks. She ignored the thought that it was a shaky confidence.

'I assume Shane's introduced himself,' said Brad, halting opposite her. 'He'll be my witness.'

'Are you paying him, too?' Kelly mocked.

'This is Kelly James,' Gwen said hurriedly. 'She's—my witness.'

'Much against my better judgment. You haven't changed any, Brad.'

His blue eyes chilled. 'I don't remember you,' he stated deliberately, looking her up and down.

'I'm not one of your ex-girl-friends, if that's what you're implying. I am, however, related to one.'

'K.J.——' Gwen began.

'My mistake,' Brad cut in with a silken taunt. 'I do remember you—the red-headed termagant. Your sister's name escapes me, though.'

'I'm not surprised!' snapped Kelly.

Gwen gripped her friend's arm. 'Kelly, you promised not to interfere.'

'So who's interfering? I'm simply making polite conversation.'

'If that's your polite side, I'd like to hear you being rude,' Shane Michaels drawled in open amusement.

Gwen spoke up before Kelly could turn her guns on this new target. 'It's eight-thirty. Could we—get it over with?'

'By all means.' Brad motioned to a short little man waiting discreetly in the background. 'This is Mr Lovell, the marriage commissioner. Mr Lovell, this is Gwen Shaughnessy and the other witness, Kelly James.'

The five people took their places before the fireplace. The location was Shane's idea. Despite his evident reservations about this loveless marriage, he seemed to

be finding some humour in the situation, and even
ribbed Brad about the lack of a carnation in his
buttonhole. A shade of annoyance passed across Brad's
controlled features, but other than that he ignored his
friend's remark, merely signalling the official to begin.

Gwen felt sudden panic rise up in her. This was it.
The marriage was really happening. Her mind erupted
into turmoil. She could still stop it. That agreement
she'd signed couldn't *make* her marry Brad. They were
not two companies merging into one holding. Business
was one thing, people another. People. Her sister and
niece and grandparents. Oh, God, what should she do?
They needed her help. And Brad didn't even like her.
And what about her career? Her principles?

From a distance, Gwen heard herself giving the
correct responses, her voice subdued, at times almost
inaudible, her outward appearance giving no sign of the
agitation within her. A slight hitch occurred when the
commissioner asked for the ring. Brad's face darkened
for an instant, then he was removing his signet ring and
taking Gwen's cold hand. His fingers were warm on
hers and she wanted to clutch at them, wanted to halt
this travesty of love and commitment before it went any
further. But amidst all Gwen's confusion and distaste
was a dim awareness that she was fighting more to keep
her heart safe from Brad's possible trampling than out
of ethics or dedication to her future career. And
perhaps it was some flicker of acknowledgement that
she would risk this danger for love that kept her silent
as the marriage commissioner spoke the final words
that would legally bind her and Brad together.

Finally it was over, and too late to stop.

'Er—if you will all now sign your names . . .'

That last chore accomplished, the commissioner was
free to leave, which he did quickly and with great relief.
There was a short silence after his departure, broken by
Brad.

'I have to get to the office,' he said, glancing at his
watch. He withdrew two items from his pocket. 'Here are
your set of keys and your bank passbook. The advance
and first month's allowance are already in your account.'

Gwen took them from him automatically. I'm married, she thought numbly. To Bradley Michel Robilliard, a handsome stranger who has absolutely no interest in me whatsoever except as a means to achieve a badly needed loan. She managed with difficulty to pay attention to what her new husband was saying.

'You and your friend here can move your things in any time. The guest room upstairs is all prepared. I'm going out of town this afternoon, so feel free to make yourself at home. Come on, Shane, let's go.'

'Hold it, buster,' commanded Kelly.

Brad turned, his expression conveying his dislike at being addressed in that manner. Kelly marched up to him and stood with hands on hips.

'For your information, I have to get back to Victoria to attend my afternoon classes. That means I won't be able to help Gwen move. That means *you* have to help her.'

'Kelly, please!' Gwen said urgently, her friend's alarming words yanking her out of her daze. 'I don't need any help, really.'

'Yes, you do. And if this man has any consideration at all, he'll help you move.' Kelly walked back to hug her. 'I'm leaving now. Call me this evening, will you? And if,' she added pointedly, without looking at Brad, 'you have any trouble with this fancy groom of yours, let me know, and I'll deal with him personally.'

'Hear that, Brad?' Shane murmured wickedly. 'You'd better watch your step.' He picked up his topcoat from the couch. 'I'll drive you to the bus depot,' he offered Kelly, eyes dancing.

'I'll take a cab,' she refused.

The two of them left, each determined on winning the little tussle. Gwen slid an uncomfortable look at Brad. 'Kelly was wrong. I can manage by myself. I only have a few things and——'

'If you only have a few things it won't take long to move them, will it?' Brad was coldly angry, but little of it showed on his face. 'Let's get a move on, I don't have all day.'

It was a silent drive to Mrs Talbot's house. As Brad started to get out of the car, Gwen stopped him.

'Please, could you wait here? I only have a small suitcase. It'll just take me a minute to get it.'

He shrugged and settled back into his seat. 'As you wish.'

Gwen hurried to her basement room. There was no way she was going to make herself beholden to Brad. The rest of her belongings could wait until she came back later with the rent she owed her landlady.

'Ha! And where do you think you're goin', young lady?'

Startled, Gwen spun to see the old woman emerging from the storage closet. Good grief, had she taken to spying secretly on her tenants now? 'Mrs Talbot, I'm——' she began.

'Tryin' to sneak out on me, that's what you're doin',' her landlady accused. 'Well, I suspected as much. I wasn't born yesterday, no siree. Where's my money, girl?'

Gwen shifted her hold on her small suitcase. 'I'm going to pick up my cheque at eleven, Mrs Talbot. That's when it will be ready.'

'A likely story! I'm not blind. That's a suitcase you got there. You were tryin' to get away without payin' me.'

'No, I wasn't. I just ... I'm moving to a different place and all I'm taking right now is this one suitcase. I'll collect the rest when I bring the money I owe you.'

'Movin'! *Movin'!*' The old woman showed alarming signs of going off into a fit. 'And not givin' me any notice, neither! That's against the law, girl! You give me one month's notice or a month's rent! Tryin' to rob me, you are. But I wasn't born yesterday You give me four hundred bucks or I'll call the cops!'

Gwen stared at her in dismay. She'd forgotten all about giving notice. Her only thought had been to rid herself of this place as quickly as possible. 'Mrs Talbot, I'll pay you the money, I promise. The moment I cash my cheque I'll come right back——'

'You're lyin', girl. I can see it in your eyes.'

'What's the hold-up?' an impatient voice demanded. Both women turned as a tall figure picked its way through the dim light afforded by the dirty windows. 'In case you're not aware of it. I *am* in a hurry,' Brad said

acidly to Gwen. He took the suitcase from her
unresisting fingers. 'Are you coming?'

'I'll be with you in a minute,' she said agitatedly. She
didn't want him to even guess at her financial situation,
or to see how she lived. 'If you'll just go back and wait
in the car I'll——'

But Mrs Talbot wasn't about to let this prize get
away. 'Oh, no, you don't. If you won't pay me my
money your rich boy-friend will. Else I'll call the cops on
you both. And don't tell me you don't have no money,'
she warned Brad. 'I saw that car you drove her home in
last Thursday. You got plenty of dough, all right.'

Brad glanced from Gwen's flushed face to the old
woman's indignant one. 'I'm not her boy-friend, I'm
her husband,' he said coolly. 'Perhaps you can explain
the trouble to me in a more reasonable manner.'

'It's none of your business,' Gwen told him. 'Mrs
Talbot, I——'

'So you're her husband, are you? A likely story! But
whatever you call yourself, I got money comin' to me,
and I want it right now.'

'Mrs Talbot, I said I'll have it for you later this
morning and I *will*.'

'Liar! I don't believe no story of cashin' your cheque
from work. You're a liar and a thief, girl. Do you hear
that? A liar and a thief!'

Gwen took an involuntary step backward as the
angry accusation was hurled at her. She felt Brad's free
arm encircle her shoulders and draw her in securely
against his side.

'If Gwen says she'll pay you, Mrs Talbot, then she
will. However, as you seem to doubt her honesty, tell
me what the amount is and I'll give you the money.'

'I can pay her myself,' said Gwen in a strained voice.
Her thigh, hip and upper arm were pressed against
Brad's hard body, picking up his heat and setting
something inside her to simmering. She tried to pull his
hand away, but it only bit deeper into her shoulder.

'Four hundred bucks, that's what it is,' the landlady
said forcefully. 'I don't run no charity house here, and
that little thief——'

'I suggest you keep your personal comments to yourself or you'll end up with no money at all.' Brad's tone was icy, his eyes a glittering blue. 'What's this four hundred dollars for?'

The woman was cowed, but not completely. 'Two hundred bucks for the September rent plus another two instead of a month's notice.'

'You've got to be kidding!' Brad had not failed to note the rundown interior of the basement. 'I have a feeling the Rentalsman's Office would be interested in the rent you're charging your tenants, Mrs Talbot.' He set down the suitcase and released Gwen to pull out his wallet. 'Here's three hundred dollars. That's all you get.'

The mention of the Rentalsman's Office had caused the old woman to change colour. Rather than argue and risk receiving an unwanted visit from them, she took the cash held out to her and retreated to the safety of the stairs. 'Make sure she takes the rest of her stuff with her,' she called blusteringly. 'I don't want none of her junk left behind.'

Brad eyed Gwen measuringly. 'I thought you said you had only one suitcase.'

'Look, I don't want to bother you——'

'You already have. Which room is yours?'

He was obviously not going to leave until he'd finished dealing with her tiresome affairs. Defeated, Gwen let him inside her room. It was a depressing place. There was a narrow bed in the corner, its bed linen worn and frayed. A wooden box beside it held a shadeless lamp. Opposite was a sorry-looking table and chair. Next to the door stood a battered chest of drawers painted a garish pink. A large suitcase, a sturdy travelling trunk and half a dozen cardboard boxes were piled up against one wall.

'Charming,' Brad remarked somewhat grimly. No wonder the girl wanted money, if this was where she'd been living!

'It looked better when I had my things out,' Gwen told him, her voice holding a slightly defensive note.

'Nothing could make this dump look better. How the hell did you eat without a fridge or even a hot-plate?'

'I managed,' she answered evasively.

'Not very well, from the look of you. You're as thin as a rake.' He swept another disgusted glance around the room, then moved towards her belongings. 'How did you expect to get these boxes over to my place by yourself?' He gave the trunk an experimental nudge with his toe. 'And this, too. It must weigh a ton.'

'I would have——'

'——managed. I know. You're an independent little cuss, aren't you?' He squatted to pick up a large box. 'You take the lighter ones. And if I find you trying to *manage* a heavy one, I'll drop it on your head!'

It took several minutes to load everything into the car, and when the task was completed Brad's suit had acquired a few dirt marks, as had Gwen's.

'I'm running late, anyway,' he muttered, sliding behind the wheel. 'Changing my clothes won't make much of a difference.' He'd also have to stop at the bank for more cash. '*Damn*,' he muttered aloud, and was further irritated when he saw Gwen wince beside him.

Back at the apartment complex, Brad commandeered the maintenance man's help and the job of unloading was accomplished much more quickly. He left Gwen to start unpacking and returned a few minutes later in a different suit to find her still looking about her new room.

'If anyone from the office calls after I've left, tell them I'm on my way,' he ordered briefly, and disappeared from the doorway.

'Wait!' She ran after him to hover uncertainly in the open area below the foyer. 'How long will you be out of town?'

'Two weeks. Why?'

'I was just . . . wondering, that's all.'

He raised an eyebrow, but all he said was, 'Don't have any wild parties while I'm away, will you?'

The door closed behind him and Gwen was left alone in her new home, listening to the echo of his rapid departure and slowly rubbing the spot where his hand had seared an imprint into her shoulder.

CHAPTER THREE

THE two weeks of Brad's absence went by quickly for Gwen, the first time in months. With her marriage to him, a monstrous burden seemed to slip from her shoulders, and she suddenly felt beautifully free, especially after she'd sent the twenty-thousand-dollar advance and her first month's allowance to her grandparents, with a slightly untruthful account of how she came to be married.

Satisfied that a dent was finally being made in the massive pile of hospital bills, Gwen turned her attention to herself. Now that there was lots of food available, she went back to eating three square meals a day, with plenty of healthy snacks in between. Up early during the week to attend classes, she was often in bed again before nine in the evening. More than anything else, this extra sleep was responsible for her improving appearance. Slowly, the dark circles beneath her eyes faded and disappeared. She had the energy now, as well as the time, to care for her hair and her body. She dug out her cosmetics case and spent an entire evening experimenting with her make-up. She painted her nails and laughed at the admiration with which she studied the end results. She tried on all the clothes she had had packed away, played music on the stereo, sang to herself as she worked about the apartment, discovered the building's pool and took up her favourite exercise of swimming. She was like a flower unfurling vulnerable petals, soaking up the sunshine so long awaited, half afraid that it wouldn't last nearly long enough.

The apartment, too, fell prey to her new energy. It was a luxurious suite and expensively furnished. To the right of the two steps leading down from the foyer was a large storage closet. Next to it were the double swing doors which led to a kitchen that included a breakfast nook and all the modern conveniences. A pantry and the laundry-room branched off this, as well as the back door through which one passed to reach the sun-deck. There was also a dining-room with its large oak table and eight matching chairs. It overlooked the living-room below, and also led on to the sun-deck.

Across from the kitchen was a wide arch leading to Gwen's room and adjoining bath, a smaller third bedroom, the main bathroom and spacious linen closets. The lower level, with its high ceilings, oak-panelled walls and large picture windows, was given over to the living-room and the master bedroom. A terrace flanked the far end of the living-room, set one level below the sun-deck.

Gwen found the entire decor ultra-modern and far too formal for her taste, so she promptly set about making the suite more comfortable and welcoming. Ornaments were whisked out from her stash of belongings and placed around the living-room. Out of the final pay-cheques from her two jobs, she bought several plants and set them at various spots throughout the apartment. Afghans were thrown over the crushed velvet sofas and armchairs, and small cushions with crocheted covers were scattered generously among them. Her grandmother wrote to say that she had used some of the money Gwen sent her—a very tiny amount—to ship a few items of her parents' furniture to Gwen. When they arrived, she used them to make the third bedroom into a den, and it was here, among furniture she had grown up around, that Gwen spent most of her free time, gaining solace from having just a part of her parents' lives with her.

On the second Friday following her marriage, Brad did not return home as she had expected. Gwen dragged about the apartment all evening, scolding herself for feeling disappointed but unable to shake a certain longing to see him again. She went to bed and lay listening for a long time to the silence around her. On Saturday, she busied herself with housework, laundry and baking, knowing that she was only passing time as she waited hopefully for the sound of the front door opening.

Sunday morning had her picking uninterestedly at her breakfast, her appetite non-existent. There could be any number of reasons why Brad hadn't returned yet— he'd simply decided to extend his trip, he was staying with his girl-friend for the weekend, he'd been in an accident and was lying in the hospital. Sighing, Gwen took her orange juice out to the sun-deck with her where the sunshine would chase away her dark imaginings. She had barely cleared the overhang when something landed heavily and sharply on her shoulder. She dropped the glass and danced around in a near panic trying to remove the furry bundle from her back. When she finally dragged it free she found it to be a big, fat kitten, and she stared at it in astonishment.

'Well, for goodness' sake! Where did you come from?'

The kitten hissed at her, but seemed disinclined to twist out of her grasp. Gwen looked up and saw a second kitten balancing precariously on the rail of the sun-deck above hers. Even as she gasped in anxious dismay, a burly, red-faced man was grabbing the kitten from its perch. He leaned over and saw the other one in Gwen's possession.

'I'll be right down to get that little monster!' he yelled.

Gwen cuddled the kitten to her breast, murmuring endearments to it as she walked through the apartment to the front door. The kitten seemed none the worse for its fall, and in fact had settled down quite comfortably in her arms.

'You're a cute little thing, aren't you, sweetheart? Poor kitty, falling all that way. It's a good thing you had me to land on.'

A series of banging knocks fell on the door and she opened it to find the red-faced man confronting her, the second kitten clutched under one beefy arm.

'I'll take him now. Sorry to trouble you. Come here, you brat!'

Gwen swerved away from his reaching hand. 'What are you going to do with him?' she queried.

'Take him to the Animal Shelter. He's been a regular terror right from the start.'

'I can't believe that,' said Gwen, studying the innocent-looking whiskered face upturned to hers. 'What have you been doing to him? The poor thing fell from your sun-deck trying to get away from you.'

'The poor thing *jumped* from my sun-deck, and I haven't been doing anything to him. It's what he's been doing to me. But I've had enough of him, wife or no wife. Out he goes, and this one, too.'

'Oh, please, I'll take him.' Gwen's gaze went to the orange kitten he was holding. 'I'll take both of them, all right?'

'Lady, you don't know what you'd be letting yourself in for,' the man warned. 'That one divebombs everything that moves and this one is constantly into trouble. A pair of devils, that's what they are.'

'Nevertheless, I'd love to have them. Please, may I?'

The beseeching look in her green eyes was hard to withstand, and the man didn't even try. 'Okay, it's your funeral.' He shoved the other kitten at her. 'I'll bring down all their food and gear. I sure as hell won't be needing it any more. Next time my wife wants a pet, We'll get a bird!'

Half an hour later Gwen and her two new kittens were ensconced on the kitchen floor, Gwen with a fresh glass of orange juice and a slice of toast, the kittens with their faces deep in a bowl of cream.

'Poor babies! You're both starved,' she said worriedly.

Then doubt came into her expression. They didn't look starved. The bigger one—Bomber, she'd named him—looked almost too well fed. She reached over to stroke his fluffy grey and white back. Perhaps they just hadn't had breakfast yet. Max stopped feeding to blink at her and she petted him, too, just to make sure each got equal attention. The thought that Brad might not be exactly thrilled by the addition of two animals to his household belatedly crossed Gwen's mind, and she was still considering methods of gaining his acceptance when he arrived home a few minutes later—under escort.

'Shane! What's wrong? What happened?' She hurried

forward to help Shane Michaels manoeuvre a weaving
Brad down the two steps from the foyer.

'He'll be all right. Let's just get him downstairs and
into bed.'

Between them, they guided Brad to his room. His
head lifted from his chest as they approached the bed
and he tried to drag to a halt.

'This isn't my office. Where's my desk?'

'You won't be seeing your office for a while, Brad old
boy,' Shane told him rather grimly. 'Come on, lie down
before you collapse again.'

'Shane, is he drunk?' Gwen asked uncertainly.

'Partly drunk, mostly exhausted. He's been working
twenty hours a day, seven days a week, for I don't
know how long now, and it's finally caught up with
him. Go wait in the other room. I'll help him undress
and be with you in a minute.'

Gwen closed the door quietly behind her. So Brad,
too, had been pushing himself past the limit. She paced
restlessly in the living-room, waiting for Shane to come
out. When he did it was with a satisfied look on his
face.

'He's asleep, and I hope he stays that way for a
month.'

'You mentioned that he collapsed,' said Gwen,
walking with him back upstairs to the foyer. 'Where
was this?'

'At my place. He'd just got in from Toronto and
dropped by to see me. The next thing I knew he was
slumping to the floor, hitting his head on the hallstand
in the process. I took him to the hospital to have him
examined, but there's just a bump on his head—nothing
to worry about.' Shane opened the door. 'His main
trouble is exhaustion, Gwen. When the human body
can't take the pace any longer it simply closes up shop,
even on tough dynamos like Brad. This business deal he
was working on in Toronto these past two weeks was
the final straw.'

'Shouldn't his own doctor take a look at him?' Gwen
asked in concern.

'He'd say the same thing I'll say, and probably get

cursed for it, too. Tell Brad that I said he's to stay
home for at least one week or I'll have him in the
hospital so fast he won't know what hit him. Rest and
relaxation are what he needs now—no worries, no
pressure, no crises. No sports or driving, either.' Shane
surveyed Gwen with smiling appraisal. 'But he just has
to look at you to realise the benefits of several good
nights' sleep and proper meals. You look terrific, Gwen.
Everything all right now?'

'I'm fine, thank you.' She fidgeted with the
doorknob. 'How did you know things weren't all right
before?'

'Just by looking at you. It was all there in your face.'

'Do you think Brad knows?'

'Brad is my best friend, but even I'm not allowed
behind that mask of his very often. And it is a mask,
Gwen. Take it away from him if you can and you'll see
what I mean.' A quick glance at his watch had Shane
edging farther out into the corridor. 'I'll phone you
tomorrow to see how he's doing. Talk to you then.'

He strode down the corridor whistling, wishing he
could be there when Brad woke up. The man was in for
one hell of a shock, that was for sure. Maybe this
marriage wouldn't be such a bad thing for him after all.

'Bomber, if you climb up that curtain one more time
I'm going to throw you out the window!' Gwen
threatened, shaking the spoon she was holding, for
emphasis.

The grey and white kitten was uncowed, merely
leaning over to give his brother an experimental swat on
the head with a sheathed paw. Max ducked automatically and continued to look expectantly up at Gwen.

'No, this is my lunch. You've already had yours.' She
picked up one of the sponge balls which their former
owner had given her and tossed it under the kitchen's
swing doors. 'Go play with that and let me eat in
peace.'

The kittens gone, she went back to the table in the
breakfast nook to finish her soup and sandwich. This
was her third meal since Brad's return yesterday

afternoon and still he had not emerged from his
bedroom, although she had heard his shower running a
few hours earlier.

Gwen stirred her soup abstractedly. Now that Brad
was home, she was nervous of meeting him again,
wondering if she had successfully ousted her flutter of
attraction to him. She certainly hoped so, because she
was set on carving out a career for herself, and she had
learned from experience that romance and ambition did
not mix. The trouble was, she kept remembering the
brief glint of humour in Brad's eyes that day in the
restaurant, and it prevented her from completing the
self-brainwashing programme she'd set up against him.
And that left a great big gap in her line of defence.

The clock in the living-room chimed one. Gwen
gathered up her dirty dishes and quickly washed and
dried them before going to look for the kittens. She had
to leave for the first of her Monday classes and figured
it would be a good idea to lock the pair in the laundry
room to keep them out of trouble while she was gone.

A thorough search of the apartment failed to locate
them, and finally with misgiving Gwen approached
Brad's room. The door was standing slightly ajar. She
knocked lightly, hesitated, then poked her head inside.
Brad was sprawled on his back on top of the rumpled
bedcovers, clad in slacks and an unbuttoned shirt, his
feet bare and hair still damp. He'd obviously showered
and tried to dress, but hadn't been able to remain
awake long. Gwen's gaze bounced off the naked
expanse of his chest and she withdrew her head hastily.

Don't be silly, she admonished herself. He's decent.
Just go in there, have a quick look around, and come
out again.

Cautiously, she slipped into the room, one eye on
Brad's sleeping form. There was no sign of the kittens,
so she started looking under and around objects with
what she hoped was great silence. She checked the
adjoining bathroom, then tiptoed carefully back across
the carpet to the wide double bed and crouched down
to search underneath.

'You won't find any money down there.'

The voice was low, mocking, and it prompted a burst of activity. Gwen jumped up, lost her balance, and fell against the bed just as a grey and white ball of fur dived from the top of the nearby window curtains and landed with particular accuracy on Brad's bare chest. He shot to his feet with a startled oath and stood holding his attacker out before him with such a hilarious expression of incredulity on his face that Gwen collapsed to the carpet again in a peal of laughter.

'What the *devil*! Where did this thing come from?'

'The ... the curtain rod,' Gwen managed to say through her laughter. 'Oh, lord, Bradley, you should have ... seen ... your face!' She doubled up again.

Her use of his full name attracted an irritated glance. '*Will* you stop laughing——'. He broke off abruptly, seeing her fully for the first time. Then long strides brought him around the foot of the bed and he was yanking her up with a painful grip on her arm. 'What the hell happened to you?'

Gone was the drab little mouse he had married. Red cotton jeans and a red and white striped top clad a slender figure with casual neatness. A narrow red ribbon held back the satin wings of her black hair from her face. Natural colour tinged her cheeks, a pale gloss had been applied to her lips and black mascara accentuated the wide green of her eyes. Rested and unworried, well fed and nicely dressed with just a touch of make-up, Gwen was a remarkably pretty girl, a fact that totally stunned Brad.

'Me?' she said, taken aback. The hilarity was replaced with bewilderment. 'Nothing's happened to me. I'm fine. Bradley, you're hurting my arm!'

He released her with contempt. 'I can see how you've been spending your new wealth. It must have cost a bundle to make the physical transformation from peasant to princess.'

She stared at him blankly. 'From ...?' The full import of his words struck her, and incensed, she took a hasty step forward. 'For your information, Bradley Michel Robilliard, these clothes, *and* the make-up, and even the conditioner I use on my hair were in my

possession before I ever laid eyes on you. And also for
your information, how I spend the money you pay me
is none of your business and I see absolutely no reason
for you to *make* it your business. And you can give me
back my kitten, thank you!'

She grabbed Bomber from him and draped the kitten
over her shoulder. Knowing perfectly well that he was
now under Gwen's protection, Bomber turned his head
and gave Brad a taunting hiss. Annoyed, Brad shifted
his attention back to Gwen.

'This is my home, and I will not allow that animal to
share it with me!'

Bomber flattened his ears menacingly and Gwen's
lips twitched. Before she could speak, however, Max
suddenly appeared out of nowhere to pounce on Brad's
ankle and begin a spirited ascent up his expensive
slacks. With a muttered curse, Brad disengaged the tiny
claws and grimly handed the climber over to Gwen,
who was choking back laughter.

'I sincerely hope I'm not about to be further savaged
by any more of your feline friends,' he said, an ominous
light in his eyes.

'No, no, there are only the two.' Gwen lifted her chin
out of reach of Max's licking tongue. 'The man above
us gave them to me yesterday.'

'Well, you can just give them right back to him.'

'He'll take them to the Animal Shelter. Oh, please,
Bradley, may I keep them? Look at these faces! They're
so cute, so adorable, so angelic, so——'

'I get the message,' he said testily. His frowning gaze
wandered over her features. 'How did you come to be
talking to the man upstairs?'

'I was out on the sun-deck and Bomber jumped down
on me from the next sun-deck up. That's why I named
him that. He's always climbing the curtains and
jumping on to people.'

Brad turned away. 'Break him of the habit or he's
out the door. What time is it?'

'Past one o'clock.' Gwen couldn't help herself—she let
her gaze roam over Brad, finding him to be exactly as she
remembered him. Tall, blond, handsome ... sexy. Too

sexy, which answered her question about that flutter of attraction. 'How are you feeling?' she asked quickly, trying to change the direction her mind was taking.

'Rotten, if you must know,' he replied cuttingly, stripping off his shirt and reaching for a fresh one from the closet.

Gwen backed hurriedly towards the door as Brad drew on the shirt and then started to unfasten his wrinkled slacks. 'I hope—I mean, you're not planning on going to the office, are you?'

'Is there some reason why I shouldn't?'

'Well, Shane says——' Gwen turned her back as the slacks came off, but not before she'd seen the white jockey shorts he was wearing. She felt the blood rushing to her cheeks and with annoyance heard Brad's voice mocking her.

'Is your maidenly virtue offended, Gwen? Too bad! You could always leave the room, you know.'

'I will, but I have to give you Shane's message first. He says you're suffering from extreme exhaustion and need to rest. He says no office, no driving, no sports— just rest and relaxation.'

'I haven't got time for Shane's nonsense.'

'He *says*,' Gwen continued with determination, 'that if you don't stay home for at least one week he's going to throw you in the hospital so fast you won't know what hit you.'

Brad pulled on another pair of slacks and tucked his shirt into the waistband, a black expression on his face. Shane would do that, too, damn him. Finger-combing his rumpled hair into some semblance of order, Brad crossed his room to hold open the door.

'Out,' he ordered Gwen. 'And take those little terrorists with you. What's *that* doing there?'

A plant set against the wall outside his bedroom had caught his attention. Indeed, it could hardly fail to do so—it was almost as tall as he was. Gwen joined him in the doorway.

'It walked in,' she said innocently. 'Well, how was I supposed to stop it, Bradley?' she asked at his smouldering look. 'It's bigger than I am.'

'Don't fool with me, Gwen. I detest plants. How many more are there?'

'I haven't counted,' she replied tartly.

Brad took a single step out and halted abruptly, having caught sight of his new living-room. 'You *have* been busy while I was away,' he commented in a voice of dangerous calm. 'Not only did you change your appearance, but my whole damn apartment as well.'

Brad pulled a colourful afghan off an armchair and flung it on to the carpet at her feet. 'I have no intention of being surrounded by junk like this. Regardless of the fact that we're married, Gwen, you are a guest in my home and nothing more, so you can just take your damn afghans and everything else and restrict them to your own room.'

Gwen rescued the afghan from the carpet and slowly balled it up in her arms, realising only now how presumptuous she had been. 'Bradley, I . . . I know I shouldn't have made all these changes without consulting you. I just . . . You were gone, and the apartment was so big and cold that I . . . I guess I just got carried away trying to make a home for myself. I'm sorry.'

Brad looked at her sharply, and what he saw in her face prompted a stab of regret for his rough words. 'Gwen, we'll compromise, right? You can have the third bedroom to use as a den or something.'

She hesitated, then, reluctantly, 'It's sort of a den already. I didn't think you'd mind, since you weren't using it, anyway.'

'Why should I mind?' he asked sardonically, all hint of softness gone. He walked over to the portable bar and poured himself a drink, mentally cursing himself for letting her curious air of vulnerability get to him. 'Is my room next on the agenda, or am I allowed to keep it as it is?'

'I wasn't going to touch it. Bradley, the den looks really nice. I've fixed up a corner for each of us and—— '

'I don't want a corner,' he said disagreeably. 'And I don't want this junk in my apartment. Get rid of it.'

'They're not junk!' flared Gwen, giving way to a

temper not entirely alien to her. 'They're afghans and pillow cushions and ornaments and pictures and plants, and they make this room look warm and comfortable.'

Brad drew in a sharp, angry breath. 'Now you listen here. I expected you to look after this place and that's it. I did *not* expect to see your sweet little domestic touches ruining my living-room or to find my furniture all rearranged, or kittens hanging from the curtains——'

'Well, what a hypocrite!' Gwen exclaimed indignantly. 'I *can't* make the apartment a little more cosy, but I *can* see that it's kept clean and tidy. How very generous of you!'

'For the amount of money I'm paying you, it's the least you can do,' Brad snapped.

'Oh, no, Bradley. You're paying me to stay married to you for one year and *that's* it. Whether I choose to do anything else is up to me.'

'I get it. You just want to laze around and spend my money, right? It's easy to see who got the better deal.'

Contempt laced his voice. Clearly he thought she was out to squander the lot. On what? Shopping sprees? Gambling? Incensed, Gwen picked up one of the maligned pillow cushions and threw it at him. It caught the hand holding his glass and he ducked back with a curse as the liquid slopped over his fingers to the carpet below.

'Who did you have to clean up after you before me, Bradley?' she demanded belligerently. 'And you must have had someone. I can't see you doing your own housework.'

'I had a housekeeper come in each day,' he snarled, grabbing a cloth from the bar to wipe his hand.

'Is that so?' she taunted. 'And I suppose you let her go upon your marriage to me, thinking that sweet little Gwen would take over the job?'

He shot her a look of dislike, rapidly revising his opinion of her. 'You're not sweet.'

'No, and I'm not stupid, either. We're sharing the apartment, so we also share the chores. Next week it's your turn to do the cleaning.'

He tossed the cloth on to the bar and confronted her with eyes of ice blue. 'I have enough to do at the office without coming home to wash floors!'

Gwen assumed an aggressive stance, hands on hips, angry colour in her cheeks. 'Oh, really? And what about me? I attend classes all day and work hard to get top marks. That means studying for a couple of hours each evening, not to mention several more hours on the weekends. So just what makes you think I have time to do your share of the chores as well as my own?'

Brad shook out a cigarette from the pack lying on the bar and lit it with suppressed anger. 'All right, you've made your point,' he grated. 'I'll have Mrs Underhill in again starting next Monday.'

'Bomber will probably ambush her and she'll refuse to return.'

Surprisingly, an order to get rid of Bomber did not follow. Instead, Brad dragged on his cigarette before saying with irritation, 'I thought you were shy. And *quiet.*' Leo's words. Damn, but he'd have something to say to his uncle when next he saw him!

'I'm only sticking up for my rights, Bradley.' Gwen studied him suspiciously for a moment to see if he'd continue the argument. When he didn't, she too let the matter drop, satisfied that she'd put him on the right track where their mutual household obligations were concerned. Obviously, he'd just needed to be made aware of what was unfair, that was all. Gwen was pleased with his quick acceptance. It showed broad-mindedness and augured well for their coming year together. She dug out a folded cheque from the pocket of her red jeans and joined him at the bar, all her anger dissipated and her usual even disposition back in place. 'By the way, here's the three hundred dollars I owe you. I want to give it to you before I leave for classes.'

Brad barely glanced at the cheque she was holding out. 'Keep it,' he said shortly, and reached for his glass again.

'I don't want to. It's yours.'

'Gwen, if I take that cheque I'm just going to tear it up, so why don't you save me the trouble by doing it yourself?'

'I owe you this money, Bradley, and——'

He set his glass down with a bang, ripped the cheque out of her hand and tore it cleanly in two. 'Let that be the end of it.'

'Bradley——' she began.

'Look around you, Gwen. Does it seem to you that I really need the money?'

'No, but I'm not giving it to you because you need it. I'm giving it to you because I *owe* it.'

'Oh, sure. You give me three hundred dollars and it comes back to you as part of next month's five thousand dollar allowance. So why give it to me at all?' Brad drained his glass and drew the whisky bottle towards him.

Gwen sighed. Lord, he was stubborn! She slid up on to the end bar stool and propped her elbows on the bar. There was something very comfortable about being here with Brad instead of anywhere else she could have been, and she was loath to leave. 'Shane didn't say it, but I don't think he wants you to drink, either.'

'Don't try to run my life, Gwen!' snapped Brad.

'I was merely pointing out——'

'Don't.'

She was silent for a moment, unruffled by his rejection of her advice, her thoughts busy. Frowningly, she broached a matter that had been puzzling her. 'Bradley, if your company was in financial trouble and you needed a lot of money to save it, why didn't you give up this expensive apartment and sell things like your car and your stereo system to raise some extra cash? You don't seem the kind of person to borrow money except as a last resort.'

'Why do you call me Bradley?' he asked softly, watching her over the rim of his glass.

Gwen blinked. 'Why do I what?'

'Everyone else calls me Brad. Why don't you?'

'I don't know. The marriage commissioner used your full name throughout the ceremony and I suppose I sort of latched on to it. I didn't even realise I was calling you that. I'm sorry.'

'Don't be,' he said briefly, and unexpectedly set glass

and whisky bottle to one side with a fleeting expression of distaste. 'Ten years ago an old man who believed in me loaned me a large sum of money to start my own business. Five years later he matched that sum so I could expand. His only condition was that I should not pay him back a cent until the tenth anniversary date of Robilliard Enterprises, at which time the entire amount became due and payable or my company became his. It was his way of motivating me to succeed.'

'So what happened?'

Brad studied the glowing tip of his cigarette. 'I succeeded. And Walter Krieger's five hundred thousand dollars was embezzled by my accountant a week before the tenth anniversary date. And my agreement with Walter was now in the hands of his son.'

'Oh, Bradley!' Gwen breathed in dismay. 'So you had only a week in which to raise all that money. You must have been desperate.'

'Desperate enough to marry you,' he said, sliding her a cool glance.

Gwen leaned back as smoke from his cigarette wafted into her eyes. 'Not me—any woman,' she corrected, waving her hand back and forth to clear the smoke away from her. 'All you wanted was to be married so you could collect that loan from your uncle.'

'That's all I thought I wanted.' His gaze raked her face, wandered lower, lifted again to settle on her mouth. 'Maybe I was wrong,' he murmured. What the hell, he might as well enjoy a wife while he had one.

His words and tone, holding the faintly suggestive ring to them, jolted Gwen into a total awareness of their relationship. This was no longer a relatively unknown stranger whom she happened to live with. He was her husband, and that put their short acquaintance on an immediately more personal level. She backed mentally away from him, striving for distance. There would be only one reason for Brad becoming interested in her, and she had no intention of providing him with any bedroom entertainment, whatever her own desires might be.

'Have the police been able to find out anything on

the whereabouts of your accountant?' she asked, meeting his eyes with attempted casualness.

'No.' His mouth tightened and he placed his cigarette in an ashtray to pour himself another shot of whisky. 'They say they have a few leads, but nothing substantial.'

'Bradley, I want to thank you for——'

His smile vanished. 'I don't want your gratitude,' he said harshly.

'Fine. I won't give it to you, then, if that's the way you feel.' Gwen pushed the ashtray farther down the bar. 'Your cigarette smoke is bothering me.'

'It would,' he said laconically.

'I hope you're not going to smoke in the den. I couldn't stand it.'

Brad stretched out an arm to retrieve his cigarette. 'I'll smoke anywhere I please. Kindly remember that this is *my* home.'

'I will, especially with you reminding me so often.' The chime clock toned the quarter hour. 'Bother, I'm going to be late.' Gwen slid off the stool with a word of excuse and ran upstairs to collect her coat and books, then came back to lean over the waist-high wall beside the stairs. Brad was still standing behind the bar, his gaze fixed moodily on the glass between his hands. 'Will you do me a favour and lock the kittens in the laundry room?' she called down to him. 'Unless you're going to keep an eye on them while I'm gone. Oh, and there are fresh muffins in the cupboard by the fridge, in case you'd like some. 'Bye—see you later!'

Gwen dashed from the apartment, a feeling of buoyant excitement lending her feet wings as she ran for the bus. Brad was back, less aloof and chilly than before, the slightest bit more relaxed with her. If he kept it up, he might just turn into a regular human being. Maybe during this next week that he was home, she could help him become one—a little teasing, shared chores, a game of Monopoly. Their basic problem was that they didn't know each other. If she could take away his mask as Shane had suggested, Gwen had a feeling that Brad would be more than worth knowing.

She gave a little skip as she reached the bus stop. Life was suddenly bright and rosy and full of fun.

When Gwen returned home early that evening it was to find the apartment as cold and quiet as it had been every day since she had moved in, and for a moment she was gripped by anxiety. Brad couldn't have left her alone again. He was supposed to stay here, take it easy. She'd gone to her classes knowing that finally she would have someone to come home to, and now . . .

She hung up her coat in the entrance closet and walked to the stairs. Maybe he was sleeping again. Maybe he'd just popped out for cigarettes. Maybe . . .

He was stretched out on the couch, sound asleep, one kitten curled up in the hollow of his shoulder and the other on his stomach. Gwen smiled tremulously. He was home. And he was going to stay.

Much more cheerful, she bustled about in the kitchen preparing supper. When it was almost ready she went back downstairs to wake her husband.

'Bradley.' She knelt to gently shake his shoulder. Bomber sat up and yawned mightily, then helped her out by placing a paw on Brad's nose. 'Bomber, don't do that! He's not too pleased with you as it is.'

Gwen transferred him and a sleepy Max to the floor, then turned back to Brad. His eyes were open and he was studying her with an unwavering regard. A hand lifted to slide beneath her hair and curve hard around the back of her neck, jerking her closer.

'Why do you look so damn different from before?' he demanded in a low, savage voice.

Gwen had fallen against his chest when he'd pulled her off balance, and for a few long seconds she couldn't move, held motionless by the breathless sensations rushing over her. Brad's chest was hard beneath her hands, his skin through the material of his shirt warm and alive. His mouth was formed in a straight line, unsmiling yet sensuous, his blue eyes twin whirlpools of smouldering sexuality. Gwen pulled away from him, clutching madly at self-preservation.

'Supper's ready, Bradley,' she said tentatively. trying

to calm her runaway heartbeat as she stood up and away from him. 'Do you want some?'

'I suppose if I eat I'll have to do the dishes afterwards.' He rolled to his feet. 'And that meek look on your face doesn't fool me for an instant. If I try to get out of doing my share of the chores, you'll probably sic the kittens on me, won't you?'

Blue eyes glinted down at her and Gwen's sense of humour asseted itself. 'Actually, I was only planning to use them as back-up. I'd *hoped* rather that your better nature would persuade you.'

'I don't have a better nature. Perhaps you should persuade me, instead.'

Gwen's smile faltered. Was he *flirting* with her? Impossible. He didn't even like her. 'I wasn't sure what you'd like,' she rushed on, 'so I'm doing steaks. Or would you prefer something else?'

'A steak would just hit the spot,' he said. 'Lead on.'

Gwen self-consciously climbed the stairs ahead of him, aware more than ever of his strong and potentially dangerous magnetism. She was beginning to think that his spending a week at home was not such a great idea after all.

During the meal their conversation covered a wide range of impersonal topics, until with the end of dessert Brad brought up the subject of the third bedroom.

'As I recall, the belongings I helped you move in here did not include two desks, a sofa-bed, and a couple of wall units. Where did you get all that furniture?'

'My grandmother sent it to me from out East,' Gwen answered after a noticeable pause. 'She thought I might like to have a few extra pieces.'

Brad rose to pour out two cups of coffee. 'She knows you're married, then?'

'Yes.'

'Does she know *why* you're married?'

'Not the real reason. Thank you.' Gwen accepted the cup he handed her, wondering what exactly she should tell Brad. 'She thinks—she and my grandfather—that it all happened so fast, that sort of thing.'

'Ah, love at first sight and straight to the altar.' Brad

poured cream into his coffee. 'And when we divorce after one year you'll no doubt tell them that you'd made a mistake by marrying so quickly.'

'Something like that,' Gwen said unhappily. She hated having to lie, especially to her grandmother. The elderly woman had been so happy for her, asking all about the groom, convinced that Gwen would only marry a man she was absolutely sure about.

'Why *did* you marry me, Gwen?' The question was soft and cold.

She shifted nervously. 'I needed—I wanted the money. I have expensive tastes,' she added more firmly.

'Yes, I can see all the jewels dripping off the plants.'

His tone was dry now. Gwen scrambled up from the table, afraid of what he might be guessing. If he knew how badly she needed his money she'd be in his power for the rest of their marriage.

'I'd better feed Max and Bomber their supper,' she said hurriedly, 'And then I have studying to do . . .'

'Those are good excuses for running away. I'll give you A for effort.'

Gwen left the kitchen in a confused state of mind. Brad was alternating between controlled anger and an almost teasing brand of mockery, and she didn't know what to make of it.

She was in the den working at her desk when he wandered in an hour later. He lowered his tall frame on to the sofa and propped his feet up on the coffee table.

'Do you mind if I sit here and read?' he asked, opening a book. 'I found a suspense novel someone gave me and I don't want to be alone, in case it gets too scary.'

'No, I don't mind.' Gwen couldn't prevent a smile. 'I just hope it doesn't give you nightmares when you go to bed.'

'If it does, you'll have to come and soothe me back to sleep.'

He *was* flirting with her. The knowledge wrecked Gwen's concentration for a good thirty minutes, during which she was minutely conscious of Brad's every movement. But as she became accustomed to his presence her nervousness left her and a comfortable silence settled between them, until at nine o'clock hunger prodded her and she got up to bring coffee and a plate of homemade biscuits into the room.

'How's the book coming?' she asked Brad, setting the tray on the coffee table.

'The hero has just discovered that someone is watching him from the closet.'

'Bradley, don't say things like that!' Gwen was glancing uneasily over her shoulder at the den's closet.

'Don't worry, Gwen, the kittens will protect us. Won't you, brat?' Bomber was poised on the arm of the couch and Brad had lowered his book to speak to him. 'Try for that plate of biscuits and you'll get your paw smacked.'

Bomber sat back respectfully, a certain understanding apparently having been reached between himself and the master of the house while Gwen had been absent that afternoon. She laughed and ruffled the furry head.

'Met your match, have you?' She sank on to her chair and reached for a biscuit. 'Bradley, you can have Bomber if you want. He seems to like you, and I've got Max after all.'

Brad tossed the book aside and returned his feet to the floor. 'You're very sneaky. Taking turns cleaning out the litter box also comes with the cat. Next you'll have me splitting the baking duties with you. These biscuits are very good, by the way.'

'Thank you. They're easy to make. Do you want the recipe?'

'Let me get the hang of changing the kitty litter before I tackle the baking.' He gave the hopeful Bomber a tiny piece of biscuit. 'What are you working on over there? It looks quite involved, judging by the stack of reference material around you.'

She sipped her coffee. 'I'm writing a report on business ethics.'

'Is that what you're studying?' Brad asked curiously. 'Business?'

'Do you find that surprising?'

'In a way. You don't seem the type.'

'Perhaps I should pull my hair back into a bun and put on a pair of thick-rimmed glasses.' Gwen retorted.

Brad was unperturbed. 'Perhaps I should change my way of thinking, instead. May I read what you've written?'

'Are you offering yourself as critic?'

'I'm interested, that's all. You don't have to show me.'

Reluctantly, she handed him her rough draft. 'Why not? I can take criticism.'

She read one of her textbooks while he silently went through the report. It left him very impressed. The girl was smart, no doubt about that. He shot a glance at her and resolved to find out more about this blushing bride of his.

'Well?' Gwen prompted a little anxiously.

'What year of university are you in?' he asked, skimming the first few pages again.

'My last.' His frowning expression was giving her a hollow feeling in the pit of her stomach. 'Is it that bad?'

'It's good and you know it. Part two, especially. You've got a sharp mind.'

'Is that surprising, too?'

Brad flicked her a brief look. 'Everything about you is surprising. What do you intend to do once you have your degree?'

Gwen reached for another biscuit. 'I've spent the last four summers working at a large marketing firm downtown and been fortunate enough to receive an offer of a permanent position with them when I graduate. And Professor Benelli, my adviser, has some connections he says he's going to make use of to get me interviews. So I hope, if my marks stay up, I'll be able to choose a job with good opportunities for advancement and success.'

'You sound very determined,' Brad observed.

'I *am* determined. Right now nothing is more important to me than my career.' *Except my family*, she amended silently.

'What about your boy-friend? Surely you have one.'

'I've decided to leave romance alone. It gets in the way of my concentration.'

'I'm glad you realise that. You have the potential to reach some lofty heights. It would be a pity if you allowed a boy-friend or lover to keep you from them.'

So Brad *had* just been flirting earlier—or perhaps teasing was the better word. Definitely, he had no desire to become physically involved with her. Gwen squashed the unexpectedly sharp disappointment this knowledge brought and told herself she was relieved. Now she could relax her apprehension that Brad would make a pass at her and let mere friendship take its course.

'Don't worry, I've learned my lesson,' she said. 'I had an offer to work in England one summer a few years back and turned it down because an ex-boyfriend didn't want me to go. And in the end we broke up, anyway. So now I steer clear of relationships. I just hope the fact that I'm married, however temporarily, won't lose me a choice opportunity.'

'And if something out of town comes up before next September, what will you do?' asked Brad with narrowed attention.

Gwen met his eyes and said evenly, 'I signed an agreement, and I'll honour it.'

He studied her a moment longer, then, 'Come over here, Gwen. I want to ask you about something on page three.'

He was back to the report again. After they'd thoroughly discussed its points, the conversation led naturally into other aspects of the business world, the two so engrossed in a subject that fascinated them both that it was midnight before Gwen thought to glance at her watch.

'Oh, lord, I should be in bed. I have an eight o'clock class tomorrow morning.' She got up from the sofa and started tidying up her desk.

'Sorry, I didn't mean to keep you up.'

She turned to see Brad placing their used cups on the tray. 'No, I enjoyed it immensely. You've given me some terrific input. Thank you.'

'You're welcome. It helped to have a good audience.' He rose with the tray balanced in one hand and two small kittens in his other arm. 'They're finally tuckered out. Where do they usually sleep at night?'

'I've fixed up a basket in the laundry room. Here, I'll take them.'

Gwen settled the pair in their warm bed as Brad rinsed the plate and cups. They left the kitchen together and paused with one accord in the wide hall.

'It's my turn to cook supper tomorrow,' said Brad. 'Do you like stew?'

'And dumplings?'

'Well, I'll try, just for you, but don't set your heart on them.'

'Okay, I won't.' Gwen tucked a wing of hair behind her ear. 'I have classes all day tomorrow. Could you feed the kittens their lunch for me?'

Brad smiled. 'I suppose I could manage such a herculean feat. What time will you be home?'

'About four-thirty or five.' The smile had drawn Gwen's attention to the firm male line of his mouth. It looked potently capable of seducing a woman with sensuous, exploring kisses. She hurriedly diverted her traitorous thoughts. 'Well, good night, Bradley. Sleep well.'

'Thank you, I will. Good night.' With an enigmatic half-smile, Brad turned and disappeared down the stairs.

Gwen prepared for bed with her thoughts in jumbled disorder. Tonight Brad had shown a sense of humour and casual friendliness that put her in as much danger of succumbing to his charm as she was of giving in to the temptation of his body. And that worried her. She could convince herself that the charm would lead to their becoming friends and that the interest in his body was merely lust, but she knew it would be a battle. Her mind was losing ground inch by inch and her heart pulling ahead. Fast. Damn, why couldn't Brad have remained unlikeable?

She switched off the bedside lamp and settled her restless body beneath the covers. The best solution of her vague yearnings was to concentrate on her studies and remember during every waking minute that she had a specific goal in life, and it was *not* to fall in love. It was a career, in capital letters ten feet tall. As long as she remembered that, she should be all right. She hoped.

CHAPTER FOUR

TUESDAY and Wednesday passed more smoothly than Monday, with Brad seemingly content to play a variety of board games, share in the cooking and cleaning, and discuss Gwen's studies with her. She brought home the materials and he built a scratching post out of wood and pieces of carpet for the two energetic kittens. And when they got into a bag of potting soil, he was the one who ruthlessly dumped them into a tub of water and soaped them clean, much to their spitting indignation and Gwen's helpless laughter.

He also had his first baking lesson, choosing as the subject an angel food cake—in Gwen's honour, he told her with subtle irony. It looked all right when it came out of the oven, but Gwen nonetheless insisted they test it on the kittens first, just in case. Max growled at his piece and Bomber, who was inclined to eat anything, walked away after one disparaging sniff. That was too much for Gwen. She cracked up laughing and teased Brad all evening about it. But she tasted the cake, and it was good.

There was one more major tussle between them. Gwen used reason and compromise and pleading, but Brad refused to refrain from smoking in the den. Finally in self-defence, she gathered up her books and the kittens and withdrew from the smoke-clouded room to study in her bedroom, instead. After a couple of hours of his own company, Brad irritably surrendered. From then on they shared the den in peaceful co-existence, Gwen not even thinking to question her husband's suddenly friendly attitude, but accepting it as a welcome change. By dint of severe talkings-to and stronger self-discipline, she was managing to regard Brad in the light of a platonic roommate, just a person rather than a man. And she was finding it a cure for her romantic leanings towards him. Just like any other familiar roommate, he annoyed her at times with some of his habits, argued over whose turn it was to do a chore next, finished the last of a food she'd been planning to eat, and criticised her at will. And she did the same with him. It led to a comfortable relationship which neither did anything to move forward or set back. They were casual friends, no more, no less. And for that Gwen was grateful. The majority of her attention, freed from diverting thoughts, could once more return to the important task of preparing herself for a successful executive career.

On Thursday afternoon, she brought home a box of paint supplies and roped Brad into helping her re-paint the laundry room a pale blue. Once the walls and ceilings were done he cleaned up to start supper, leaving Gwen to finish the wooden shelves alone. She was busy with a difficult corner when the doorbell rang. Thinking that Brad would answer it, she dipped her brush and renewed her assault on the shelf. The doorbell rang again.

'Bradley, will you get that?' she called in exasperation.

Silence from the kitchen. Muttering to herself, Gwen set her brush down and walked out to the foyer. She rose on tiptoe to peer through the peephole.

'Oh, terrific! And here I am looking a perfect mess,' she thought. She opened the door and smiled politely at the expensively dressed woman standing in the corridor. 'May I help you?'

The woman's gaze travelled insolently over her, taking in the tight, faded blue jeans and shrunken grey sweatshirt, both liberally splattered with paint. A cotton scarf covered Gwen's head, hiding every strand of hair. 'You must be the little wife,' the woman said disdainfully. 'I've come to see Brad. Is he here?'

'Yes, he is. Please come in.'

Gwen stepped back, studying the visitor as she walked regally past—tall, voluptuous, with platinum blonde hair piled high and a face made striking by make-up. Gwen wrinkled her nose and silently condemned Brad's taste in girl-friends. You're just jealous, she told herself. Three, nearly four days of

Brad's exclusive company and already you've become possessive of his time! She pulled the scarf from her head, feeling at a distinct disadvantage in her beat-up clothes.

'Brad *was* making supper,' she said aloud, hanging up the coat languidly held out to her. 'I'll go see if I can find him.'

'My dear girl, there's no need. I know my way around.'

The woman descended the stairs to the lower level and with a careless shrug Gwen pushed through the kitchen's swing doors to return to the laundry room. Brad was just closing the door to the sun-deck, two chastened kittens under his arm.

'Did they get out again?' Gwen asked needlessly. 'Bradley, you should know by now to watch for them when you open that door. How big a chase did they give you?'

'About two minutes' worth. I'm getting better at catching the little speedballs, wouldn't you say?' he set them on the floor and clapped his hands together to make them scurry off. 'I thought I heard the doorbell ring. Who was it?'

'A visitor for you,' Gwen answered, stuffing the cotton headscarf into a back pocket before hopping up on to one of the high counter stools. 'She's probably in your bedroom by now.'

He regarded her steadily for a moment before crossing over to the stove block beside her. 'What's she doing in my bedroom?' he asked, lifting the lid from a pot and stirring its contents with a wooden spoon.

'She said,' Gwen replied carefully, 'that she knows her way around.'

'Maybe it's my former cleaning lady,' Brad suggested, a ghost of a smile on his lips.

She choked. 'No, Bradley, I don't think she's that. Not unless your cleaning lady always came to work in a satin dress.'

'Ah, satin, is it? Sounds ominous. Here, taste this.'

He cupped a hand under the spoon poised before her. Cautiously, Gwen tasted the curry sauce on it, having learned to be suspicious of Brad's concoctions. She'd barely swallowed when she was waving her hand frantically in front of her mouth in a vain attempt to cool the fire sliding down her throat.

'Bradley, it's hot!' she gasped.

He was already bringing a glass to her lips, eyes dancing. 'Of course it's hot. It's been cooking on the stove.'

Her hands closed over the masculine one holding the glass and she drank half the water before letting him lower it. 'I didn't mean hot hot,' she said, wiping her mouth. 'I meant *spicy* hot. And you can quit laughing, too, or I'll——'

'Brad, did the little wife not tell you I was here?'

The voice was a whiplash, breaking in on their humour. Brad lifted another lid, unruffled. 'The little wife told me I had a visitor, but as I couldn't see one around I assumed she must have mistaken the matter.' Still not looking up, he added implacably, 'And her name's Gwen. I would advise you to remember that, Corinne.'

'Certainly, darling, anything you say.' The woman came forward, bringing with her a strong cloud of perfume and a suddenly charming attitude. 'I can see she's already ruined the tone of your apartment. Those afghans, darling, and ornaments cluttering up the place—so juvenile and tasteless! And after all the trouble I went to in decorating this delightful suite!'

And what was that little gem of information supposed to mean? Gwen glanced at Brad. Was this *really* his girl-friend? She seemed to give the impression that she was, even if he didn't.

'Gwen went to a great deal of trouble redecorating,' Brad told her, turning down the heat under his pot of rice. 'Personally, I find the change a vast improvement. It's explained to me why I never liked coming home before.'

'I'm sure you're just saying that to spare her feelings,' Corinne said sharply. 'She's even brought in plants, which I know you dislike having around.'

'A preconceived dislike prompted by my lack of familiarity with them. They're actually not that bad. And the kittens regard them as their own personal jungle, so naturally I can't get rid of them.'

'Kittens? You have *kittens*?' Corinne was plainly horrified. 'Brad, they'll ruin your furniture!'

'No, they won't,' Gwen denied. 'They run all over the couches and chairs, but they don't scratch at them, not since he made them a scratching post. Bradley, is the curry sauce burning?'

He pulled on an oven mitt and removed the pot from the hob. 'Yes, we each have a kitten,' he said conversationally, disregarding Corinne's views. 'Mine dive-bombs everything. You'd better watch your back, Corinne.'

She jerked her head around to check behind her, and Brad used the opportunity to smile at Gwen. He was obviously in a mood to bait the other woman, and deriving some amusement from her reactions. Gwen frowned, wondering if she herself was being used in this little game. This was the first she'd heard that he liked what she'd done to his apartment.

Corinne faced them again with a tight smile on her thin lips. 'Kittens, plants, afghans—you used not to be so deplorably homebound before, Brad.'

'I never used to have a wife before.'

The casual remark startled both Corinne and Gwen, its meaning unclear. Gwen met the other woman's eyes and was shocked by the ugly expression in them.

'You'll excuse us, won't you?' said Corinne with a bite to her voice. 'I'd like to talk to Brad privately.'

'Sorry, Corinne, Gwen stays. She's my guinea-pig.' Brad opened the fridge door behind him and began taking out ingredients for a salad. 'By the way, Gwen, I gathered earlier that our visitor had neglected to introduce herself to you. She's Corinne Mason, my company treasurer.'

Corinne ignored Gwen's polite response. 'Brad, I'd like to discuss a business problem with you. I'm sure the little—I'm sure Gwen would find it all very boring.'

'She's in her fifth and final year of an honours programme at university, majoring in Commerce and Business Administration, with a minor in Computer Sciences,' Brad told her. 'I don't think she'd find it boring at all.'

Gwen stared at him. How had he found that out? She hadn't told him anything about her minor or the honours classification.

'How interesting,' Corinne murmured, but it was plain that Brad's information had knocked her for a loop. The little wife was not supposed to have brains.

'At any rate,' Brad continued, taking a salad bowl from the cupboard, 'I told you on the phone that Jack and Allegra would handle any problems while I'm away from the office. If they can't, they call me themselves.'

'Fine. I'll take it to Jack. But you will be back on Monday, won't you? Or is your—illness—still with you?'

'Oh, I'm slowly getting better.' For some reason, Brad's gaze caught and held Gwen's for an instant. 'But yes, I'll be in Monday. Too much of a good thing might spoil me. Now, I can see you're dressed to go out, so don't let us keep you.'

Corinne bit her lip. 'I was hoping you might take me to dinner and the theatre. A night out would do you good. You must find it extremely boring being stuck at home every evening.'

'Not at all. There are plenty of things to do.'

Brad moved behind Gwen to casually encircle her shoulders with his arms. She tried once to pull away, but when his hold only tightened she relaxed back against his chest, her hands curved lightly around his muscled forearms, unable and unwilling to break this rare physical contact between them. Brad's breath stirred her hair as she spoke, his voice low and amused just above her head.

'Take tonight, for instance,' he continued non-chalantly. 'After we finish painting the laundry room, Gwen and I are having a Monopoly re-match, then I think I'll bake some chocolate chip cookies, and after that it will probably be about eleven and time for bed.'

'And is that something else the two of you do together?' Corinne flashed, losing her temper at the sight of their apparent closeness. 'Go to bed?'

Gwen could feel Brad stiffen. She opened her mouth to hastily deny a charge that hit too close to her suppressed fantasies, but Brad's voice came first, loaded with icy danger.

'Perhaps you could explain to me, Corinne, how that's any of your business?'

Corinne seemed to back off a mile—and fast. She gave a hollow laugh. 'I'm sorry, that was a silly question. Naturally you wouldn't . . .' Her words trailed away as she glanced at Gwen's bent head, at Brad's arms still snugly around the younger woman's shoulders. 'Well,' she made a pretence of checking her watch, 'if you're not feeling up to a night on the town, I won't push you. Good night. I'll find my own way out.'

Brad waited for the sound of the front door closing, then dropped a kiss on to the top of Gwen's head. 'I don't think she'll be asking me to take her out any more!' His arms loosened from around her, but only to draw her off the stool and against his hard length. 'Don't let anything she said bother you, Gwen.'

Corinne was the last thing bothering her. Without a word, Gwen pulled out of his casual embrace and marched back to her painting. He'd been using her to rid himself of a girl-friend he no longer wanted, and putting his arms around her had been merely for effect, not because he liked her. She cursed her own flare of hope and wished she'd thrown Brad over her shoulder or something equally karate-like and efficient. Not that she knew karate, but she would have made a darn good attempt at it. His false praise of the apartment and his proposed evening schedule deserved equal treatment.

Brad had followed her and now propped a shoulder against the door jamb, folding his arms across his chest. 'All right, spill it. What are you mad about now?'

'Your behaviour,' Gwen said tightly. 'Running on about all the fun things you're going to do this evening—baking cookies, playing Monopoly, making them sound absolutely thrilling!'

'No, they're not thrilling. Did I really make them sound that way?'

She splashed her brush in the paint tray, not answering him.

'Oh, the silent treatment. Most refreshing.' Brad was

suddenly beside her, a hand going to her chin to bring her face around. 'Listen to me, Gwen. I bake because I want to. I paint walls, feed kittens, cook and wash dishes, make scratching posts because I want to. And I play Monopoly with you because I enjoy your company.' A smile warmed his eyes. 'Besides, I'm determined to beat you at it just once.'

'And the other stuff?' she asked, hardening her resistance against his disarming smile.

'What other stuff?' he asked, wilfully not understanding her.

'You know very well what other stuff,' she accused, jerking her chin out of his grasp. 'Putting your arms around me——'

'Did that bother you?'

'Yes. You——'

Brad moved closer, his mouth a mere breath away. 'Does this?' he asked. His head started to lower.

Gwen drew back, her heart hammering in her chest. Brad was stepping outside the role she'd assigned to him, instantly setting off alarm bells inside her head. 'You weren't very polite with Corinne,' she ventured, attempting to change the subject.

'Politeness doesn't work with her.'

'Why did you let her think that we—that you and I— that we were sleeping together? Because that's what she thought, after you said what you did to her.'

His thumb brushed across her soft mouth. 'I don't know. Wishful thinking, I guess.'

Gwen stepped right back, desire shivering through her body. Oh, Lord, she actually *wanted* Brad to kiss her, longed for it with a hunger that made her tremble. Lust, she told herself shakily. It's simply lust. He's got such a *great* body. Not trusting this conviction at all, she dropped the topic like a hot potato. The situation was fraught with peril, and she needed space to think. 'Is supper ready? I'm starved!'

'So am I,' said Brad, straightening.

Somehow she got the feeling that he wasn't referring to the same thing she was.

* * *

The next morning Gwen rose with a sense of emptiness. It was her birthday today, but without her parents to share in the event, she didn't feel much like celebrating. Depressed, she skipped her daily swim and sat for a long time at the kitchen table, letting her breakfast grow cold as memories played hauntingly in her mind.

The phone rang once and she jumped to answer it before it woke Brad. The voice on the other end was shaky, but determinedly cheerful.

'Hi, birthday girl. How does it feel to turn the big two-one?'

'*Naomi?*' Gwen sat down slowly, hardly able to believe that it was her sister on the phone.

'The one and only. I'm just calling to wish you a happy birthday and to tell you that there are parcels on the way from myself and Grandma and Grandpa.'

'Oh, Naomi, I miss you,' Gwen said shakily, her eyes brimming with tears. 'How are you? Did you get the card I sent you last week?'

'Yes, I got the card, all two feet of it, and the ten-page letter inside. You talked a lot about university, Gwen, but mentioned nothing at all about this man Grandma says you married. Why not?'

'Well, after ten pages, I—I figured the rest could wait for another letter.'

'Don't give me that, Gwen!' Her older sister's voice still had a ring of authority to it, despite her physical suffering. 'You did it for us, didn't you? As soon as I heard about the big bundle of money that came in, I knew.'

Gwen played with the belt of her robe. 'I had to do it, Naomi. It was the only way I could help you. All that money . . .'

'I know. It's just—Gwen, I'm so damn helpless, flat on my back in the hospital like this, and I hate it. I can't even look after myself, let alone my daughter.'

'Grandma and Grandpa are managing her, Naomi. Just you concentrate on getting better, okay? I hear you were sick there for a while.'

'Nothing to worry about,' her sister said with false

lightness. 'A temporary setback, that's all. I'm used to them by now.'

Gwen drew her bare feet up under the warmth of her robe, worrying anyway. 'I wish I were able to visit you each day. If I hadn't come back to university this year . . .'

'You had to, honey, or you would have lost the rest of your scholarship. Gwen, I know you made up a story that would satisfy Grandma and Grandpa, but will you tell me what the real situation is with this Brad? Why did he marry you?'

'It's a bit complicated, Naomi,' Gwen sighed. 'Too complicated to go into over the phone. I'll sit down one day and write you a letter telling all about it.'

'But is he treating you all right? If not——'

'He's nice. Nicer than I first thought.' Too nice for my peace of mind, Gwen almost added. She stood up. 'By the way, how did you manage a long-distance call from the hospital? I didn't think they'd let you do something like that.'

'My doctor's paying for it,' Naomi answered, and Gwen could hear the smile in her voice. 'He says it's a reward for being a good patient.'

'Well, you are a good patient. After all you've been through——'

'And you,' her sister interrupted. 'Working your heart out to send us as much money as you could, while trying at the same time to cope with Mum and Dad's death. How are you doing in that area, Gwen?'

'I'm fine.'

'The truth, kiddo.'

'It's—still hard,' Gwen admitted with difficulty.

'Yes. For me, too. Losing Bob as well . . .'

There was a constricted silence between the two sisters, which Gwen was the first to break. 'I have to finish getting ready for class, so I'll let you go. Thanks so much for calling, Naomi. It's helped a lot.'

'It's helped me, too. Are you going out to celebrate tonight?'

'Some friends are taking me to dinner. Take care, Naomi, and hug Julia for me the next time she visits you. And Grandma and Grandpa . . .'

'I will, honey. And you take care, too.'

Gwen was feeling better when the phone call ended. Carrying her glass of orange juice with her, she went into her bedroom again to investigate the contents of her wardrobe. Why not something new for tonight? It was her twenty-first birthday today and she still had some money left over from her two final pay-cheques. A new dress, something special to really pick up her spirits. *And perhaps impress Brad?* She shook her head violently to dislodge that thought.

After her last class of the day she spent an enjoyable hour shopping, arriving home at five o'clock well satisfied with her purchases. Brad was just coming up the stairs, a cigarette dangling from his mouth and an open cookbook in his hands. Since his brief flirtation last night—and Gwen made sure to call it a flirtation, rather than anything more sincere—she could no longer look at him as a mere roommate. His move towards a kiss had torn away that illusion and had left in its place a reality that she couldn't run away from this time. It made her aware all over again of his very male presence, his lazy grace, the blue of his eyes, the way his clothes moulded to his tall, lean body, his tantalising smile, his easy capability in everything he did ... the fact that he was her husband. Gwen had spent the evening fighting this awareness, finally accepting it on the promise that she wouldn't let it disrupt her life. Now, looking at Brad after a night of firm resolve, she knew that her promise to herself was going to fall prey to a lot of testing. Starting right now.

'Hi,' Brad greeted her, with a casualness she wished she could match. 'How do you feel about beef Stroganoff tonight?'

Gwen stared at him in dismay. 'Oh, Bradley, didn't I tell you? I'm going out tonight.'

'No, you didn't tell me.' His eyes went to the parcels in her arms. 'Big date?'

'No, some friends have invited me to dinner.'

She waited, hoping that he'd remember that it was her birthday—the date had been on the marriage licence— but he merely closed the cookbook and removed the cigarette from between his lips to say coolly, 'Well, enjoy yourself. I'll see that the kittens are fed, don't worry.'

Gwen watched in disappointment as Brad went into the kitchen. She would have spent a quiet celebration dinner at home with him if he'd asked, but today's date held no significance for him and she wasn't going to give any hints.

She took her time getting ready for the evening, having a nice long bath and brushing a sheen into her newly-washed hair. Her make-up was applied with careful precision, highlighting the green depths of her eyes and accentuating her finely moulded features. She'd known the moment she'd seen the dress that this was what she'd been looking for. Its full silk and chiffon skirt swirled about her knees in varying shades of green from the palest tint to a deep emerald, while the matching bodice clung lightly to the bare skin of her upper body, held up by spaghetti-thin straps which would require the merest brush from a man's hands to slip caressingly from her shoulders. Brad's hands.

Gwen breathed deeply to steady her suddenly racing pulse. 'You'd better not start thinking like that again,' she told her reflection sternly. 'I've told you over and over again what a mistake that would be.'

Turning away from the mirror, she strapped on her new high-heeled gold evening sandals. On went tiny gold studs for her pierced ears, a delicate gold locket to nestle just above the shadowed cleft of her breasts and a thin gold bracelet to encircle a slender wrist.

There was no sign of Brad when she left her room. Slipping into her cream wool coat and buttoning it up, Gwen checked the kitchen, then the living-room. Had he gone out? The glowing tip of his cigarette drew her attention to the sliding glass doors. He was standing outside on the terrace, watching the last sunset of September. Gwen opened the door to speak to him.

'I'm leaving now, Bradley,' she called, hoping to the last that lightning would strike and he'd realise that it was her birthday.

His chiselled profile didn't change expression. 'Fine. I'll see you later.'

He was, quite obviously, not interested in whether she stayed or left. Deflated and depressed, Gwen left for a celebration she would now just as soon pass up.

Brad heard the door close and abruptly flicked his cigarette out into the evening air. He'd told Leo he wasn't the marrying kind and he'd meant it. He'd *meant* it. And a friendly pair of green eyes—beautiful, laughing, intelligent green eyes—was not going to convince him otherwise. So what if he'd never felt more content in his life? So what if he'd found in himself a liking for evenings spent at home and shared housework and cooking for two? So what if he'd had the fleeting—the very fleeting—thought that Gwen would make a terrific mother of the children he'd claimed not to want? All of that meant nothing. He was only human, and not immune to such lapses in good sense. Naturally, it went without saying that he was completely uninterested in this marriage. In a few more days he'd be bored by the entire novelty of it and not spare Gwen a second glance. Well, maybe a second one. God, she was lovely! Her looks had been there before, but had been heavily overshadowed by her dull appearance. Now she overflowed with personality, and it was becoming increasingly hard to resist the total attraction she presented.

Brad's mouth twisted in self-derision. He wasn't content. He didn't like housework or cooking or evenings at home. All he wanted was to get Gwen into his bed, and those activities were simply a means of working towards his goal. The thought left him feeling more dissatisfied with himself than truthful. Irritably, he lit another cigarette, inhaled briefly, then tossed it the way of the other. Gwen was having a bad influence on all his favourite habits. When was the last time he'd had a drink? The afternoon she'd left him at the bar in the living-room and gone off to her classes. Hell, that was four days ago.

He went inside and poured himself a whisky. The silence in the apartment was deafening. Brad hunted for the kittens and found them curled up asleep beneath an armchair. It would be mean to awaken them. He wandered into his bedroom with his drink. This was the only room Gwen had not touched with her personality. He suddenly realised how much he disliked its whole decor. Maybe Gwen would have some ideas for improving it. He'd ask her when she came home.

The living-room clock chimed six. Gwen had barely been gone five minutes. Brad set down his glass, the contents hardly touched, and left his room to go upstairs. He fiddled around in the kitchen for a while, took out a steak from the fridge freezer, put it back, considered heating up the leftovers from last night's supper, decided even that was too much effort. He got out the Yellow Pages Directory from a drawer by the phone and sat down at the kitchen table to peruse those restaurants that delivered. He didn't feel like pizza for supper. Didn't feel like Chinese food. Nor—Brad slammed the Directory closed and thrust it away from him. He glanced at his watch. Six-fifteen. Would this evening never end . . .?

It was late when the taxi dropped Gwen off in front of the apartment building, past four in the morning. Her friends waved goodbye before directing the driver onward, and she started carefully up the steps to the front entrance. The night security guard was there to open the door for her, greeting her politely.

'Good evening, Mrs Robilliard.'

She blinked at him. That was the first time he had called her by name, by—Mrs Robilliard. It sounded nice. She smiled, 'Actually, I think it's morning.'

'After four o'clock,' he agreed.

She nodded. 'I've been out celebrating my birthday with friends. They gave me a surprise party.'

'Happy birthday, then,' he said, thawing a little.

'Thank you. Good night.'

Gwen caught the lift to the fifth floor without it occurring to her that the security guard might wonder why her husband had not accompanied her on such a special occasion. Stopping before her door, she rummaged around in her evening purse for her keys, swaying the slightest bit.

'Aha!'

She pulled them out and spent several seconds trying them all before inserting the right one. Stepping inside, she locked the door behind her and wandered into the kitchen, leaving a trail of bag, coat and shoes as she went. Switching on the light, she paused for a moment to consider why she was there, then padded over to the refrigerator. There was a bowl of jelly inside, but she decided she might have trouble getting that wriggly stuff into her mouth, and passed on that. She was reaching for an interesting-looking covered dish when a familiar voice spoke with ominous calm behind her.

'A bit late getting home, aren't you?'

Gwen withdrew her head from the fridge, the dish in her hands, and turned to see Brad lounging in the doorway.

'Would you like a leftover potato?' she offered, having lifted the lid and discovered the disappointing contents of the dish.

With a slow, piercing appraisal, Brad's blue gaze travelled down the length of her body and leisurely up again to her face. 'Pretty fancy get-up for a mere dinner with friends,' he commented.

'It was a birthday dinner,' Gwen said with dignity. 'A *fancy* birthday dinner.'

'It was long, too. You've been gone over ten hours.'

'We went to a cabaret afterwards.' Gwen frowned at the dish in her hand, then set it back in the fridge. 'There must be something better to eat in here.' She opened the freezer compartment. 'Oh, good, ice-cream.' She pulled the carton out and looked vaguely around for a spoon.

'Did it never occur to you,' said Brad bitingly, 'that I might be worrying about your whereabouts? For all I knew, you could have been in an accident.'

'What accident?' asked Gwen, staring at him in bewilderment.

His eyes narrowed to make a more detailed inspection of her, and his mouth quirked. 'Have you been drinking, Gwen?'

'Certainly not!' She became aware of what he was

wearing—a short black towelling robe that left his long legs bare, its belt loosely tied so that his smooth bronze chest was partially revealed. 'You shouldn't dress like that,' she told him severely. 'It isn't fair.'

'Why isn't it?'

Because it was doing strange things to her senses, as was that husky, low-pitched voice of his. Gwen felt herself getting closer to a forbidden edge and found some measure of control by remembering her manners.

'Did I wake you?' she asked politely.

'Yes.'

'Oh. Well, I'm sorry. Why don't you go back to bed?'

Brad smiled faintly. 'Do you mind if I take you with me?'

'No. I mean, yes, I do mind.' She had a hazy feeling that she was treading on dangerous ground, and wished she had not had so much to drink. It was impairing her defences. 'Besides, I'm not tired, I'm hungry.'

'So am I.'

She offered the carton in her hands. 'Would you like some ice-cream? It's ...' she held the container at arm's length, then brought it up to her nose, 'Chocolate,' she produced brilliantly.

Brad pushed away from the door-jamb and lazily closed the distance between them. 'You're loaded, aren't you?' he asked in amusement, reaching past her to open a drawer.

Gwen decided he was much, *much* too close and backed a good four feet away from him, bumping into the kitchen table. 'Ouch!' She rubbed her hip painfully before scraping back a chair. 'I have been celebrating,' she explained, sitting down and fumbling with the flaps of the ice-cream carton.

'Celebrating a friend's birthday, I know.'

'Not a friend's. *My* birthday. My twenty-*first* birthday, which is something special.' She gave a frustrated sigh. 'Can you open this, please?'

Brad joined her at the table and handed her a spoon. 'I'm sorry, Gwen,' he said slowly, 'I didn't know.'

Her chin lifted. 'That's because you have a rotten memory.'

He reached for the ice-cream carton frowningly, then comprehension dawned. 'The date was on the marriage certificate, wasn't it?' Impatience threaded his voice as he pushed the opened carton back to her. 'For heaven's sake, Gwen, how did you expect me to remember a trivial item like that? I hardly glanced at the wretched paper!'

'I didn't expect it,' she said frostily. 'But if you were any kind of decent human being you would have remembered.' The ice-cream caught her erratic attention. She scooped out half a teaspoonful and popped it into her mouth, wrinkling her nose at the taste. 'Chocolate. Did you buy this?'

'No.'

'We had strawberry at the party. I thought my friends were just taking me out for dinner, but there must have been twenty more people at the restaurant when we arrived. And there was a huge cake with pink icing—I would have brought you a piece, but there wasn't any left.'

Brad rose abruptly and opened a cupboard to take out the kettle. He set it on the counter and then just stood looking down at it, unmoving. 'You should have told me, Gwen,' he said quietly.

She frowned, wondering vaguely if she had somehow hurt his feelings, and cast back in her mind for the gist of their recent conversation. She couldn't come up with anything. In fact, she couldn't really remember what they'd just talked about. She rose somewhat unsteadily to her feet and took the half-dozen steps necessary to join him at the counter.

'Bradley, I'm sorry you didn't come to my party,' she said tentatively.

He turned his head to look down at her and even through an alcoholic fog she could feel the shattering intensity of those bright blue eyes. A hand came up to caress her cheek. 'A birthday kiss is all I've got for you, Gwen.' He placed his other hand on the small of her back and slowly drew her body against his.

'Bradley . . .' she began uneasily.

His lips brushed hers in a featherlight kiss that set her

heart pounding. She went very still and he kissed her again, the barest touch. It was agony. She clutched at the lapels of his robe and melted into him, parting her lips for another. Hard arms gathered her slender form in and his mouth covered hers in a kiss that scorched her to the soul, igniting a fire she had been trying to prevent ever since her first meeting with Brad. She freed her hands from their entrapment against his chest and reached up to wrap her arms tightly around his neck, kissing him back with an appetite that matched his own. She couldn't get close enough to him, couldn't get enough of the mouth so expertly and thoroughly exploring hers. A part of her was shocked by this wanton reaction to finally being in Brad's arms, but the rest of her craved satisfaction of the feelings he was arousing in her. And as mouth explored mouth in hot, sweet, hungry passion, curbed desire broke free and burst into a blazing inferno, spreading swiftly through their bodies, dangerously close to raging out of control.

Caught up in its flames, Gwen was yet aware of Brad's hold on her shifting to allow his hands more freedom. The thin straps of her dress were nudged aside and sensitive fingertips caressed her shoulders. The satin they found there sidetracked Brad's burning discovery of her mouth and he transferred his attention to her vulnerable collarbone.

'Bradley!' she gasped, tilting her head to one side as his lips whispered against her skin with potent effect. She caught her breath and tried again. 'Bradley, I don't think you should be doing this.'

'Why not?' His searching lips found the pulse at her throat.

'Because I'm rather drunk and I'm . . . not quite sure . . . what I'm doing.'

'You're putting ideas into my head, that's what you're doing.' He nipped lightly at her ear.

Her hands slid down his shoulders to his upper arms. 'That's just it,' she said. 'I don't think I should be. At least, not—not tonight. I'm not thinking straight. Or seeing straight, for that matter.'

The straps of her dress slipped farther down her arms

and she felt the silk bodice begin to droop. She thought she heard Brad draw in a sharp breath, then he was raising his head to find her mouth again. She gave it to him willingly, unable to prevent herself, and at the same time felt the tantalising touch of his fingers on her bare breast. She moaned softly in her throat and arched her body against his, gripped by unfamiliar physical desire of such intensity that all rational thought was blocked out. With no experience to go on, but only instinctive need, she found and untied the belt of his robe, her hands parting the edges to slip inside and encircle his lean waist. She pressed closer to him, liking the feel of his naked skin. And suddenly Brad's mouth became rough, more demanding, his arms bands of steel around her. Drugged by the alcohol in her system, by Brad's kisses and the skill in his caressing hands, Gwen knew only that the fire in her was also in him, and that it was consuming them both in its searing heat.

'Gwen, you're my wife.'

The words, breathed against her mouth, were almost a warning, as if he were cautioning her that he was fully aroused and had no intention of letting any agreement in their marriage contract keep him from persuading her to total surrender. Gwen could feel his arousal and didn't want him to stop, but the subtle warning managed to find an unclouded part of her mind. She wrenched herself out of his arms and backed against the fridge to stare at him in confusion, her fingers fumbling to pull the bodice of her dress up over her breasts. Brad said one low, vicious swear-word and re-tied the belt of his robe with quick jerks.

'Me and my big mouth!' he muttered in furious self-disgust. He eyed her grimly. 'Quit looking so damned seductive!'

She pulled the green silk up higher. 'Don't swear at me—it's not nice!'

'I'm not feeling nice right now.' He slammed the kettle back into the cupboard. 'You,' he said harshly, 'have just shot this platonic marriage of ours all to hell.'

'You shouldn't have kissed me.'

'I shouldn't have married you,' he snapped.

Gwen raised a hand to her forehead. 'I don't feel well,' she said plaintively.

'Take a cold shower; I'm going to.'

'At this time of night?' she asked, startled.

A sardonic smile touched his lips. 'Would you rather I take you to bed with me?'

'No, I . . . I don't think so.'

'But you're not certain?'

Gwen closed her eyes to shut out the sight of his body in the short black robe. God, how she wanted him! 'You're not playing fair, Bradley,' she whispered.

He had no trouble understanding her meaning. 'Neither are you. That dress was just asking to be taken off you.'

'I bought it today.'

'It's very lovely.'

Gwen's eyes flew open to find Brad not six inches away from her, all anger gone from his face. Holding her gaze with his, he reached out and slowly drew the straps of her dress up over her slim shoulders.

'There. You can let go now.'

Her hands lowered, but only to steal to his waist as she swayed towards him. He met her halfway, his kiss gently probing, not demanding anything but the sweet nectar she was giving him. And this time it was he who drew away first, when she wanted to cling to him and never let go.

'Tomorrow, Gwen.'

'Tomorrow?' His mouth was still close and she stole another kiss. He set her more firmly away from him.

'Tomorrow we'll talk. Now say good night.'

'Good night.'

But she didn't move. Brad pulled her against him, gave her a swift, hard kiss, then propelled her over to the doorway, fighting temptation all the way.

'Go to bed, Gwen. Before I change my mind and take you to my room instead.'

With a last lingering look at him, she wandered across the wide hall. Once behind her door, she stepped dreamily out of her clothes and slipped under the blankets, whereupon any intention of thinking about what had happened in the kitchen was frustrated as she promptly passed out.

CHAPTER FIVE

GWEN awoke several hours later to pouring rain and a kingsize hangover. She rolled over on to her back, giving a loud groan of acute misery. That didn't help anything, and she rolled back to stare up at the ceiling with a woebegone expression on her face. Half an hour passed during which she considered not moving for the rest of her life, then, finally, slowly and very, very carefully, she pushed back the covers and set her feet on the floor. The realisation that she was nude and the sight of her clothes scattered carelessly on the carpet hit her at the same moment. She froze in consternation, then warily turned her head to look over her shoulder at the other pillow on the bed. There was no indication of anyone having laid his head there. Of course not, Gwen scolded herself. What was she thinking of? Besides, she would remember if such a thing had happened, and her friends would never have let her go home with a man in her condition, anyway.

She rose and somehow made her way into the adjoining bathroom. One look at herself in the mirror above the sink made her turn resolutely to the tub and turn on the shower full blast. Never, she thought with a shudder, *never* will I have another drink as long as I live!

Three-quarters of an hour later she had showered, scrubbed away all trace of the previous night's make-up from her face, washed and dried her hair, and brushed her teeth. Feeling a slight—a very slight—return to normal, she tightened the belt of her long robe and left her room to get a glass of juice from the kitchen. Halfway across the hall, she saw Brad running up the stairs from the lower level, and stopped dead. He was clad only in snug-fitting blue jeans and was vigorously rubbing his damp hair dry with a towel. Gwen's gaze skittered over the bronzed skin of his chest and

84

shoulders and she felt her pulse jump into high gear. Even as her mind and body registered his overwhelming presence, he lowered the towel and came to a lazy halt in her path, a crooked grin pulling at his mouth.

'Good morning. Or should I say good afternoon?'

'Excuse me,' Gwen said weakly, and retreated somewhat precipitately back to her room. Every other morning she had been dressed and gone before Brad awoke, and being caught today wearing only her robe and no make-up unnerved her. She looked at her alarm clock on the nightstand. Past two. No wonder he was up!

She dressed in deep pink sweat pants and a matching pullover sweat shirt. The outfit was loose, comfortable and just the thing for a rainy Saturday afternoon spent at home nursing a hangover. A touch of mascara, an extra brush to her hair, and she was ready to face anything.

Well, not quite anything. Brad, looking attractively casual in his blue jeans and a cream-white, heavy-knit pullover sweater, was cooking an omelette when she entered the kitchen, and at sight of it Gwen pressed a hand to her rolling stomach. 'Do you *have* to do that *now*?' she begged.

'What's the matter?' he asked in smiling mockery. 'Hangover can't handle it?'

'Bradley, I'm dying.' She flopped down at the kitchen table and cradled her head in her arms. 'At least cover it with a lid or something.'

'A glass of tomato juice and tabasco sauce is the usual remedy for your problem.'

'That would kill me for sure,' she said, her voice muffled.

Brad carried a plate and cup of coffee to the table and sat down across from her. 'See any pink elephants yet?'

Gwen straightened. 'No, just lots and lots of pink icing.' She viewed with disfavour the omelette and toast on his plate. He was a heartless brute to eat in front of her. She said crossly, 'It was my birthday yesterday, you know.'

'So you belatedly told me.'

Her eyebrows drew together in puzzlement. 'I did? When?'

Brad paused in the act of spreading jam on his toast to look at her with arrested attention. 'Last night, after you came home.'

'Last night?' Something stirred in Gwen's mind, a memory of sensuous passion that had been fully reciprocated. Nonsense. That had all been just a dream—the kissing, those strong arms around her. She stole a glance at Brad and found him regarding her steadily. A touch of colour rose to her cheeks. Heavens, if he ever found out that she'd actually *dreamed* about him ...

'Don't you remember?' he asked in a quiet voice.

She started guiltily. 'Remember what?'

There was a short pause, then, flatly, 'Never mind.' Strong white teeth bit savagely into the toast. He'd kill her! He really would.

Gwen set her elbows on the table and clasped her aching head between her hands. 'Bradley, I don't know what you want me to remember. I came in at three in the morning and went straight to bed.'

'It was four, not three,' he said crushingly.

She looked at him in surprise.

'You woke me up with all your stumbling around.'

'I'm sorry.' Really, he didn't have to sound so unpleasant about it!

Brad pushed his plate away and stood up, his face a set mask. 'Not half as sorry as I am, believe me.'

He strode from the kitchen and a moment later Gwen heard the front door slam. 'Well!' she muttered indignantly. '*Some*one sure got up on the wrong side of the bed this morning!'

The thought of bed diverted her mind. Tomato juice and tabasco sauce wouldn't help her, but a nap might. A nice *long* nap. She rose from the table, gave Brad's unfinished omelette to the kittens to eat, then made her way back to her room. It seemed she had hardly lain down when a hand was rudely shaking her awake. She groaned and dragged the spare pillow over her head. It was pulled away.

'Wake up! There's a phone call for you.'

'A—what?' Still half asleep, Gwen raised her head to
see Brad already leaving her room. 'Why couldn't he
just take a message instead of waking me?' she
grumbled, swinging her feet to the floor.

He was in the kitchen unpacking groceries when she
padded sock-footed through the swing doors. 'You
could have taken a message, Bradley,' she said
aggrievedly, combing a hand through her tousled hair
as she picked up the receiver from the counter. 'Hello.
Gwen speaking . . . Leo! Where are you calling from?'
The lingering traces of her hangover vanished at the
welcome sound of her godfather's voice. 'Yes, I'd love
to have dinner with you. What time? . . . No, that's fine.
See you then. Goodbye.'

'Another night on the town, I see,' Brad lashed out.

Gwen turned from hanging up the wall phone to give
him a surprised look. 'What's the matter with you?'

'Nothing.' He tossed her a box of crackers. 'Here, put
that away.'

She smacked it down on to the counter. 'Oh, I get it,'
she bristled. 'You're still carrying around a grudge just
because I woke you up coming home late last night,
aren't you?'

'You woke me up, all right,' he admitted grimly. 'It
took me hours to get back to sleep again.' He sliced her a
look of bright steel. 'And it's not a grudge I'm carrying.'

'Well, what is it then? You're certainly mad about
something.'

His mouth tightened. 'That's an understatement.'

'Okay, don't tell me.' Gwen shrugged, and headed for
the doors. 'My godfather's in town and he's taking me
to dinner for my birthday, so I'm going to change.
Enjoy your bad mood!'

Brad's voice followed her with ripping anger. 'Stick
to milk this time, will you, Gwen? Drink takes you way
out of your league!'

She pivoted to face him, her hair swinging out from
her shoulders in a heavy swish of black satin. 'And just
what is that supposed to mean?' she demanded hotly.

'It means don't play with fire!' snapped Brad, slamming a cupboard door shut on some tinned goods.

Thoroughly riled now, Gwen snatched up the gauntlet he'd thrown down. 'If you're referring to my state of inebriation, Bradley,' she said furiously, 'just come out and say so! One thing you're not is polite!'

'Oh, forget it. Let's just drop the subject, okay?'

'No, not okay! You started it and you're going to finish it! Now what's your problem? I go out, have a good time——'

'I'll *bet* you had a good time!' he cut in savagely. 'Was the whole party one big drunk? Dancing on tables? Strip-tease acts? A little cuddling in dark corners? And don't give me that look of outrage. You're not as innocent as you like to pretend. That act when I first met you, and later at the marriage ceremony here—the hair pulled back, the cute little blushes, no make-up, the tasteless clothes. I don't know what kind of stunt you were trying to pull, but——'

'No stunt!' she exploded in boiling wrath. 'I don't pull stunts! I don't dance on tables! I don't do strip-tease!'

'Cut the pretence, Gwen.' Brad's words dripped sarcasm. 'Are you going to say next that you don't have a few lovers around, an experienced little kisser like you?'

She breathed in sharply at his insult. 'You despicable, lowdown, arrogant——! What have you been doing, listening to fictitious gossip? Is that how you get your thrills?'

'That last piece of information I got from a very reliable source. And it's fact, not fiction. You're a very good kisser.'

Infuriated and wounded by his unprovoked attack on her, Gwen spat venom back at him. 'Fine. *Fine!* You're so damned interested in my affairs, ask me what I've done with the money you've given me so far. The twenty-five thousand dollars. Go ahead, ask! Never mind, I'll tell you! It's gone, every penny of it. There, are you happy now? I went on a spending spree to end all spending sprees. And while we're on the subject, I'd like an advance on next month's allowance. A thousand will do. I'm throwing an open house party next Friday for all my friends and——'

'You . . .!' Brad swiftly crossed the room and grabbed her roughly by the shoulders, looking down into her startled face with barely leashed fury. 'You are driving me right up the wall, Gwen, do you know that? *Right up the wall!*'

He pushed her away from him and went back to putting the groceries away, his anger silent and cold. Gwen rubbed her bruised arms, watching him with a trembling lower lip. Their easy camaraderie was gone, ripped apart by quick tempers, insults and lies. She felt as if she'd lost a friend, and amidst the emotional debris their fight had left behind, wondered in distress if in fact she had actually ever had one.

'I must be a boring conversationalist. This is the second time your mind's wandered this evening.'

'What? Oh, Leo, I'm sorry.' Gwen reached across the restaurant table to clasp her godfather's hand contritely. 'It's my fault, not yours. You're never boring.'

'Problems, Gwen?' he enquired with sympathetic interest.

She glanced away, avoiding his shrewd eyes. 'No, everything's fine.'

Leo gave her hand an affectionate squeeze before releasing it. 'Have I told you how much better you look since the last time I saw you?'

'Several times.' Gwen smiled, returning her gaze to his.

'Studying must be good for you.'

'It keeps me busy, yes, along with other things.'

'Less time to think about your parents?' he asked gently.

Gwen ran the tip of her forefinger around the rim of the glass holding her after-dinner liqueur. 'Not as much as I used to, at any rate. It helps to be living with someone el——' She broke off in confusion and cast a quick glance at Leo. He was regarding her questioningly. She took a sip of brandy, uncertain whether to tell him about Brad. Her godfather had always been an important figure in her life—encouraging her to fulfil her dreams and ambitions, checking up on her welfare each time he visited Vancouver on business, taking deep pride in all her achievements. He had been in Europe when Gwen's parents and brother-in-law were killed, and one of his first actions on his return a few months later was an offer of money. Gwen had refused it, knowing that Naomi and her grandparents would never accept charity, like them preferring to work together to pay off the accumulating debts. What would Leo say when he learned that after turning down his offer she had almost jumped at taking Brad's?

'So you have a roommate, do you?' he was saying casually. 'By any chance would it be the man who answered the phone when I called?'

Gwen continued to hesitate, then suddenly took the plunge. 'I'm married, Leo. Sort of. I mean, I am legally, but it's not a real marriage. Brad—my husband—had to marry quickly in order to get a lot of money he needed, and I receive some of that—the money—for staying married to him for one year.' She searched his face anxiously, but with his usual self-control he was showing no reaction, not even surprise. 'I did it for my family——'

'I know.'

'You *do*?'

'What I mean,' Leo said carefully, 'is that I know you would never agree to such an arrangement unless there was a good reason, and your family would be it.'

Gwen fidgeted with the bracelet which had been his birthday gift to her. 'It's so much easier than accepting your offer of assistance, Leo. This way it's money earned rather than charity.'

'It's a large amount, I take it?'

'A hundred and fifty thousand dollars,' she answered, still unable to believe it herself. 'Plus Brad pays all my living expenses—rent, food, that sort of thing.'

'Very generous of him. And how do the two of you get along?'

Gwen's expression became slightly wistful. 'We were doing all right until today.'

'Oh?' Leo's glass halted halfway to his lips. 'What happened today?'

'We had a fight,' she sighed. 'He was in a bad mood to begin with—why, I don't know—and after I talked to you on the phone he lit into me.'

Leo's gaze sharpened. 'He wasn't unkind to you, was he, Gwen?'

'Of course not! Brad isn't an unkind person. He simply dreamed up some story about my being a good-time girl and then decided to take it personally. And,' Gwen added darkly, 'got in a few cheap shots while he was at it. Even if I was like he described, my social life is none of his business.' She dwelt resentfully on Brad's iniquity for a moment, then became aware of her godfather's tactful silence and grimaced. 'I'm doing it again, aren't I?'

Leo smiled. 'Your husband seems to be heavy on your mind. I—exchanged a few words with him before he called you to the phone this afternoon. He mentioned that you'd been out until all hours of the morning celebrating your birthday.'

Gwen wrinkled her nose. 'That's a sore point with him, too. He said I woke him up when I came in. And just as I was leaving the apartment, he said to tell you to bring me home at a decent hour. Bossy, isn't he?'

Secret amusement seemed to shake Leo. 'It's another good sign,' he observed, almost to himself, and changed the subject before she could ask him to explain his comment. 'I arranged for someone to join us after dinner. He's just arrived.' Leo was already rising to greet the man approaching their table. 'Trace, glad you could make it. I'd like you to meet my god-daughter, Gwen Shaughnessy.'

Gwen shook hands with the tall, darkly handsome stranger and watched frowningly as he sat down in the extra chair brought by an attentive waiter and ordered a drink. Leo had neglected to say Trace's last name, which was frustrating in a way because there was something decidedly familiar about the newcomer's face, especially his eyes, but without knowing his full name she was finding it difficult to place him.

'Dinner ran on longer than I expected and I'm afraid I have to leave to catch a plane,' her godfather was saying out of the blue. He came around to Gwen's chair to kiss her cheek. 'Trace will look after you and see that you get home at the decent hour demanded.'

'But, Leo——'

'I should be seeing you again some time next month, Gwen.'

'Yes, all right. Leo, wait! Thank you again for the gift. And for dinner . . .'

'You're welcome. Remember, Trace, a decent hour—orders from on high!'

His departure left a short silence behind. Trace was studying Gwen with the coldest eyes she'd ever seen, their arctic blue holding absolutely no expression. And when he spoke his voice, too, was chilly, emotionless.

'Leo's strategy is not what it used to be.'

Gwen was not dumb. 'Are you implying that he deliberately left us alone together?'

'When I met him for lunch today he mentioned that he was staying the night in Vancouver.' Trace pulled out a slim gold case and offered her a cigarette, lighting one for himself when she shook her head in refusal. He exhaled a stream of smoke and surveyed her through narrowed eyes. 'I don't like being manipulated, Miss Shaughnessy. Leo knows that, yet he still arranged for us to meet. Now why do you suppose he did so?'

'I have no idea,' she answered stiffly. 'My godfather sometimes chooses to do things for what he thinks is my own good, without consulting me. Perhaps you're one of them.'

'Then he's out of his mind; I'm no good for anyone.' It was an indifferent remark, with no hint of a bid for sympathy. Trace knew exactly what kind of person he was and seemed undisturbed by it. He tapped ash from his cigarette and, if possible, his blue eyes became even colder. 'Are you by any strange coincidence the Gwen Shaughnessy whom Joseph Benelli has been filling my ear with all afternoon?'

Gwen looked her surprise. 'Professor Benelli is my university adviser.'

'So you're the one! You look extremely young to be in your fifth year of the business programme.'

'I just turned twenty-one. I also skipped a grade back in elementary school.' Curiosity pricked her. 'Why was Professor Benelli telling you about me?'

Trace shrugged. 'I run the Dragonar Corporation. He thinks you'd be a decided asset to the company.'

The Dragonar Corporation! Gwen nearly stopped breathing. To be one of the few business graduates selected each year to join that mammoth company! She carefully set her glass down on the table.

'And what do you think, Mr—Trace? I assume you've checked me out.'

'You have a brilliant track record, both from high school and at university. Academically, yes, you're a potential candidate. But you're young. And inexperienced.'

'Professor Benelli wouldn't have bothered you with me if he didn't think I had the capabilities to fulfil all your expectations,' she said quietly.

'Joe Benelli and I are old friends, so I'm quite aware of that. It's on his recommendation that I'm offering you a position with my company on your graduation next spring.'

Gwen only just managed to contain an exclamation of glee. Such a display would be to her detriment in the eyes of her future boss. She would undoubtedly have to cultivate some sophistication next year!

'Thank you,' she smiled. 'I can't tell you how much this means to me.'

'I'll see how much it means by how hard you work,' said Trace, unaffected by her gratitude.

He got down to details then, telling her what to expect at Dragonar and discussing her present work at university. In the middle of all this, Gwen again felt the flash of familiarity and unthinkingly interrupted him.

'I don't want you to take this the wrong way,' she said cautiously, 'but I have the strangest feeling that we've met before. *Have* we?'

'No.' He flicked a burning glance over her, in that one look stripping away her clothes and making her feel naked. 'If we'd met, I would have made sure you'd remember it.'

Gwen put up her chin. 'Meaning you would have tried to get me into bed?'

'I would have tried, yes. You're a tempting little package.'

'Well now, this is a pleasant surprise.'

The voice was neither pleasant nor surprised, but it was definitely familiar to Gwen and she looked up quickly. Her immediate reaction on seeing Brad was one of warm pleasure. Then she remembered the terms on which they had parted and her welcoming smile disappeared.

'I beg your pardon?' she said haughtily.

'Not too much of a surprise, Brad,' Trace spoke up, leaning back in his chair. 'You knew I was coming to town this weekend to discuss business with you.'

Gwen's startled gaze jumped from Brad to him. 'You two know each other?' And then she saw it. One was fair and the other dark-haired, but their eyes were the same electric blue, and when the two men were seen together the family resemblance was unmistakable.

'Unfortunately, yes,' Trace replied in answer to her question. 'Gwen, this is my brother, Brad Robilliard. Brad, Gwen Shaughnessy.'

Hard blue eyes slammed into Gwen's. 'Shaughnessy, is it? Odd, but I somehow pictured you as having a different sort of name. French-Canadian origin, perhaps.' He pulled out the chair recently vacated by Leo and lifted it around to Gwen's other side. 'I'll join you two for a drink.'

'I don't recall inviting you,' Trace said icily.

'Your memory is as sharp as ever,' Brad responded, and then to the waiter who had appeared at his elbow, 'Scotch on the rocks, please.'

The chair had been set noticeably close to Gwen and when Brad sat down his knee brushed against hers under the table. She hastily shifted her legs away, glancing at Trace as she did so. His expression was controlled, but when he spoke his anger was evident.

'Back off, Brad! Gwen is with me.'

'My dear brother, you can't expect to keep this lovely young woman all to yourself,' Brad chided. 'Besides, you never talk anything but business and I'm sure she's dying for a fresh topic of conversation. Do you like animals, Miss Shaughnessy?'

Gwen stared pointedly ahead. So he was going to play games, was he? Fine, then so would she. 'I loathe animals,' she stated succinctly.

'Do you really?' Brad nodded his thanks as his drink was placed before him and continued blandly, 'I'm quite fond of them myself. I have a kitten—or had. Unfortunately, he went missing around suppertime.'

Gwen whipped her head around in sharp concern, saw the taunting look in his eyes, and berated herself for being hooked in right away. 'The poor thing probably had enough of your scintillating company,' she said disparagingly.

'Possibly.'

Brad's gaze made a lazy appraisal of her clinging white dress, its long tight sleeves and high, straight neckline accentuating slim curves rather than revealing them. The dress was one of Gwen's favourites and she felt as if it were being slowly, sensuously slipped off her body by those deliberately probing eyes. She became indignant.

'Stop that right now, Bradley! You're just doing it to annoy me, and it won't work.'

'No?' He reached out to brush an ebony strand of hair from her cheek, his fingertips a featherlight caress. 'I said some rotten things to you this afternoon, for which I deeply apologise. I was angry and didn't mean any of them. Will you forgive me?'

His words instantly erased that scene from Gwen's mind as if it had never happened. With a readiness that told her how anxious she was to get back on their old terms, she took Brad's hand in both of hers to examine the flash of red she'd seen, by her action conveying her unspoken acceptance of his apology.

'You're really becoming battle-scarred,' she said, a rueful smile curving her lips as she looked at the long scratch on the back of his hand. 'What was it this time?'

'Sheer cussedness. Ever since that bath, I've been at the top of their hate list.'

'Poor Bradley.' Gwen suddenly realised that the game was over and turned her head to see her brother-in-law lounging back in his chair, watching them expressionlessly. 'Trace, I'm so sorry for ignoring you. We ... I ...'

'Don't mind me,' he said with a faint shrug. 'I saw the light the moment Brad mentioned a kitten. It was obviously a familiar subject.'

'We each have a kitten,' Gwen remarked, releasing Brad's hand to reach for her brandy, 'and both act like they own the whole apartment.'

Trace's gaze zeroed in on her in sharp surprise. 'Do you two live together, then?'

She coloured. 'Well, actually——'

'Gwen is my wife,' stated Brad with cool exactness.

'Your wife!' Trace was not one to react visibly, but this information plainly staggered him. 'Leo didn't say a word about any marriage!'

'I only told him tonight at dinner,' Gwen explained, and to Brad in explanation, 'Leo is my godfather. He's the one who introduced Trace to me.'

A strangely intense look shot between the two brothers and Trace sat up slowly. 'Just what the hell is going on, Brad?'

'Nothing that's any of your business. Is this a birthday present from your godfather?' Brad was lifting Gwen's wrist from the table, his eyes on the fine gold chain with its diamond chips set at spaced intervals.

'Yes, isn't it beautiful? He said that a twenty-first birthday deserves something special.'

'The old man doesn't know about this, does he?' Trace said softly.

Brad let go of Gwen's wrist, but merely to link his fingers loosely with hers. 'No, and he's not going to.'

Gwen was only faintly aware of the sharp warning in Brad's voice, her senses too wildly scattered by what he was doing to her. He had shifted in his chair so that his shoulder was brushing hers, and she could smell the highly disturbing male fragrance of his shaving cologne, could reach up if she wanted to and run her fingers through his fair hair. And his touch—he was absently playing with her fingers, his skin warm and intimate against hers.

She tried unsuccessfully to pull her hand free, not wanting to feel this tingling of her body, the way her pulse leaped at the intimate contact of Brad's flesh on hers. She was reaching for that first rung of the corporate ladder, and couldn't—*wouldn't*—get romantically involved with a man. Any man. Not yet. Especially such a powerhouse of intensity as Brad. He would burn her up and then leave her cold, taking her heart and all her spirit with him.

Realising this, Gwen reaffirmed her resolution and flashed the word career in her mind several times. Brad's thumb stroked the sensitive skin of her palm and immediately the word career was replaced with mental pictures that tempted her resolution sorely. She fought them with all the determination that had got her to an honours level in university and placed her on the receiving end of Trace Robilliard's magical offer. The pictures faded slowly, and relief flooded through her. She'd won—this time. But it had been close. The battle between what her mind wanted and what her heart needed was heating up. And Gwen wondered uneasily which side she was really on.

'You can't have been married long,' Trace was saying thoughtfully. 'When I saw you two months ago, you were dating a brunette and marriage was the farthest thing from your mind.' His cold eyes ran over Gwen, but this time there wasn't a hint of sexual interest. 'I must say, your taste has improved dramatically. I think even the old man would be in favour of Gwen's addition to the family.'

'Philippe's opinion is of no interest to me, and hasn't been for thirteen years.'

The words were spoken indifferently, but Gwen saw a nerve twitch along Brad's jawline and sensed that he was holding some powerful emotion in check. She closed her hand around his with instinctive reassurance and felt his fingers tighten. 'Is Philippe your father?' she asked, looking from one to the other. 'You referred to him as the old man and——'

'Our grandfather,' Trace replied, and dragged on his cigarette, watching Brad. 'He wants you to come back to Toronto and help me run Dragonar.'

'Does he?' Brad enquired mockingly. His voice flattened out to a savage bite. 'It'll be a cold day in hell before I go anywhere near Philippe and his cut-throat methods of rearranging my life. Tell him that, with my compliments.'

Trace's gaze slid briefly to Gwen. 'Judging from what I've seen, you've no need to worry about your wife. She's not anything like Pamela.'

'I'm not worried,' Brad said tersely.

He drew Gwen's hand down under the table to rest intimately on his thigh, his action seeming to be an unconscious one of protection. She glanced from him to his brother, thoughts jostling for space in her mind. First and foremost was the rapidly blossoming idea that Brad actually cared for her, and not just as a friend. This was curbed a little by the reference to Pamela—a former girl-friend who had possibly meant a lot to Brad?—and lingering doubts about his relationship with Corinne. And Dragonar. She remembered now. The Eastern company was a large multi-million-dollar enterprise founded over fifty years ago by a shrewd and ruthless businessman named . . . Gwen went very still. The Dragonar Corporation had been founded by Philippe Robilliard. And Brad was his grandson. The floor seemed to rock beneath her feet.

'How's Kristin?' Brad asked his brother. 'Have you seen her lately?'

'I saw her last week in Paris. Don't you think it would be a nice idea to let her know she has a new sister-in-law?'

'It's a private affair, Trace. The only reason I let you in on it was because you were trespassing on my territory.'

Trace regarded Brad coolly through a cloud of smoke. 'She was off limits to me, anyway.'

'Calling her a tempting little package didn't sound

like you were treating her as off limits,' the other said thinly.

'For God's sake, Brad, she's Leo's god-daughter!'

'So? That might make you hesitate, but it wouldn't stop you.'

'Then put a ring on her finger, dammit, because that sure as hell would!'

Gwen's objection to their talking about her as if she wasn't there collided with the pleasure Brad's possessiveness gave her, both fading as premonition gripped her. 'Bradley?' she said apprehensively. 'Do you know Leo, too?'

'No, I don't,' he replied curtly. Irritation was in the glance he flicked at his brother. 'Trace, would you mind putting out your cigarette? The smoke bothers Gwen.'

She paid no heed as Trace leisurely butted the cigarette. 'But the way you were talking——'

'I know my brother. He'd think twice about making a play for his friend's god-daughter, then he'd overcome his twinge of conscience and do his best to seduce you.' Brad picked up his drink, his hooded gaze meeting his brother's. 'Trace, you see, has no morals to speak of.'

'Neither do you,' Trace said softly, meaningfully. Faint amusement appeared in his eyes. 'Just for the record, Leo isn't a friend. He's—a business associate. You should meet him, Brad. I'm sure the two of you would find much in common.'

Gwen turned impulsively in her chair to face her husband, unconsciously carrying his hand to her lap. 'Oh, Bradley, that reminds me! I have the most fantastic news! My university adviser was talking to Trace earlier today and after Leo left he—Trace, I mean—asked me to join the Dragonar Corporation when I graduate next spring. Isn't that wonderful?'

There was a lengthy silence. Brad and Trace were looking at each other again, the former grim and cold, the latter quietly watchful. The brightness began to fade from Gwen's face.

'Bradley?' she said uncertainly. 'Aren't you pleased for me?'

'No, I'm not,' he said shortly, transferring his hard

gaze to her. 'Dragonar is a corporate monster. It'll eat you alive.'

'I'm tougher than I look——'

'You're nowhere near tough enough to go up against my esteemed grandfather.' Brad's eyes cut back to his brother. 'You can't have her, Trace.'

'Bradley, it's my decision,' flared Gwen, contrarily angered by his possessiveness now. 'You have no say in the matter!'

'I have one year's say,' he snapped, 'and while you're married to me you won't go anywhere near Dragonar.'

'I won't, anyway,' she said in a low, furious voice, flinging his hand away from her. 'I've already told Trace that I'm not free to leave Vancouver until next September, so you can quit worrying that I'm planning to renege on our agreement.'

'This marital argument is completely unnecessary,' Trace remarked laconically. 'Gwen, in view of your relationship with my brother, I'm rescinding my invitation for you to join Dragonar.'

She jumped up. 'What has *that* got to do with it?' she cried. 'Being married doesn't affect my qualifications for the job!'

'Being married to Brad does, however.'

She turned on her husband. 'You *see*? I told you this would happen!' Grabbing her clutch purse, she strode swiftly away from the table.

'Don't you think you'd better go after her?' Trace frowned.

'She'll take a taxi home and the security guard will make sure she gets in safely. If I went with her she'd only throw something at me.' Brad raised his brooding gaze from his glass. 'Thanks for nothing, Trace. You've been a great help.'

'If I'd known she was married to you, I never would have offered her the job. You know that, Brad.'

'And what am I supposed to tell Gwen? She's a top student with a remarkable flair for business. When I talked to her university adviser the other day he couldn't speak highly enough of her. She deserves only

the best offers, and in her eyes Dragonar is certainly the
best of the best.'

'Tell her the truth,' Trace suggested.

'No.'

'Brad, if she really pushes it, she could bring a charge
of discrimination against me, and in the end she'd be at
Dragonar, anyway. Hell, I saw the way you were with
her. If Philippe sees it, too—and he will, because he
never misses a trick—it'll be the Pamela episode all over
again.'

'Gwen's not like that.'

'Then why are you so adamant about keeping her
away from the company?'

Brad was silent. He was beginning to know his wife,
but there was still a long way to go. She had married
him for money. Would she divorce him if a greater
amount were offered?

'Brad.'

Trace's voice was soft, the glacial demeanour which
so often made strangers uneasy warmed a little by the
deep attachment between the two brothers. They'd been
through a lot together in their early years—they and
Kristin, their younger sister. Years of growing up as
orphans under the uncaring dominance of a grandfather
who chose to ignore a mere girl and tried to mould two
boys into his own image. It had left a bitterness and
distrust which Brad only now realised he was hoping
Gwen might help erase. His wife. His funny, unquiet,
independent, provoking and extremely desirable wife.
To have someone like her loving him ... Brad gave
himself a mental shake. He didn't need her, didn't want
her except physically. She was a nuisance, shackled to
him by her doting godfather. He couldn't wait for the
year to be up. Even if she did make him laugh. And
feel. *Damn* her for not remembering last night!

'Brad, Pamela wasn't worth the pain she caused you,'
his brother was saying. 'But if Philippe gets his hooks
into Gwen and she believes whatever lies he tells her—
are you willing to risk losing her like that?'

'It would certainly show which way the wind blew,
wouldn't it?' drawled Brad, reaching for the other's

cigarette case. 'Do you mind? Gwen won't let me smoke in the apartment.'

'And you're trying to pretend you don't care about her?' Trace mocked. 'If she meant nothing to you, you wouldn't pay any attention to her objections.'

A grin flashed briefly across Brad's face. 'If I didn't pay strict attention, she'd sic our pair of terrorists on to me.'

'Married life obviously suits you,' commented Trace drily.

'There are some aspects of it I've yet to experience,' was the dry response.

'Like fatherhood?'

The question wiped all sign of humour from Brad's face. He stood up, saying abruptly, 'You were always rather bright, Trace. Don't tell me your intelligence has suddenly deserted you.'

'All right, so the marriage was arranged. Gwen is Leo's god-daughter, she obviously doesn't know that he's also our uncle, you needed money to keep your company out of Howard Krieger's hands, Leo apparently loaned you that money since you didn't come to Dragonar and I haven't heard of your getting the financing from any other source, you have a one-year agreement with Gwen—yes, I've added it all together and come up with a good guess. But that doesn't mean it can't turn into something special.'

'You're a fine one to talk!'

Brad led the way to the cashier and paid the bill. When they were outside, Trace said with faint worry, 'Don't become like me, Brad. You and Kristin are the only two people I care about. The women in my life don't mean a thing to me, and never will. I only wish one of them could. But it's not too late for you. Let Gwen love you. And love her back. It would do a lot for my peace of mind if I knew you were happy.'

'And what about your happiness?' Brad asked quietly.

'Me?' Trace gave a short laugh. 'I wouldn't know what to do with love if it hit me in the face. That's why I've never got seriously involved with a woman. I think

I'd only end up hurting her too much.' He raised his hand to motion for a cab. 'Go home to your wife, Brad. And tell her I said "Welcome to the family".'

CHAPTER SIX

GWEN rose early on Sunday morning, only to find a note from Brad saying he would be out all day and P.S. he'd fed the kittens. Her intention of having a rousing fight with him frustrated, she spent the entire day and most of the evening cleaning the apartment from top to bottom, rehearsing everything she was going to say to Brad and getting a vicarious satisfaction from imagining his abject apologies, pleas to be forgiven and promises to do anything she wanted of him. Sensing her boiling mood, Max and Bomber were prudent enough to keep out of her way

She was up on a kitchen chair washing windows when Brad came home that night. The radio was playing loudly beside her, and the first warning she had of his presence was when two steel hands gripped her waist and swung her to the floor. She landed off balance and had to clutch at him for support.

'Bradley! You startled me!'

He held her at arm's length, admiring the slim-fitting white overalls over a bright yellow T-shirt. 'I've had a rough day, Gwen. Kiss me better.'

It was an alluring prospect. No, it *wasn't*. Gwen remembered her quarrel with him and pulled away. 'Stop flirting with me, Bradley. I know you don't mean it. And why have you had a rough day? You're not supposed to go back to work until tomorrow.'

'I had to take care of some business with my brother.' He stooped to pat Bomber, who had been batting at his trouser leg for attention.

'And how was the rest of your evening with Trace? You certainly got in late enough.'

Brad straightened to send her a penetrating glance. 'How do you know what time I got home? I checked on you and found you fast asleep—or so I thought.'

The idea of him watching her as she slept shook

104

Gwen. Last night she had worn skimpy baby-doll pyjamas to bed, and after all her tossing and turning before getting to sleep, the disordered covers must have revealed at least half an eyeful to Brad when he had entered her room. Rather than raise a possibly embarrassing subject, she took refuge in going on the attack. 'You woke me up with all your stumbling around!' she informed him aggressively.

'I wasn't drunk, so I wasn't stumbling. You're pushing for a fight, Gwen. Why?'

She threw the wash-rag into the pail of soapy water, unmindful of the resultant splash. 'You dare to ask why! You lost me one terrific job, Bradley!'

'I had nothing to do with that,' he said evenly. 'Trace doesn't want his sister-in-law working at Dragonar. It would smack too much of favouritism, and the resulting jealousy could be vicious.'

'I could handle it. And I wouldn't be his sister-in-law when I arrived. We'll be divorced by then.'

'Ex-sister-in-law. Same thing. And you'll still have my name.'

'I'll change it back to my own!' Gwen flung at him.

'Rumours spread,' Brad shrugged. 'They'll still learn that you were married to one of the Chairman's grandsons.'

'You just don't want me to be a part of your family company, do you?' she accused, hurt by this realisation. 'And you made sure I wouldn't be by telling Trace outright not to hire me.' The phone rang and Gwen hurried to grab up the receiver so Brad wouldn't see the sparkle of tears in her eyes. 'Hello.'

'Hello, Gwen, it's Leo. Sorry to be calling you so late, but I just got out of a long meeting and wanted to say goodbye to you before I left town.'

'I thought you left last night, Leo,' she demanded.

'Er—no, I found myself delayed—business, you know.'

'Oh. Well, where are you off to now?'

'New York.' Her godfather's voice changed. 'So, did Trace get you home all right last night?'

'No, he didn't,' Gwen said shortly. 'Brad showed up,

and after losing me a wonderful job opportunity, he stayed there talking to Trace while I went home.'

'What job opportunity?' Leo asked sharply.

'With the Dragonar Corporation. Then my *husband* came along and ruined everything.' Gwen's gaze swung pointedly to Brad. 'I'll *never* forgive him for it!' He smiled sardonically at her and she abruptly turned her back on him.

Leo seemed to draw in an impatient breath. 'That's just great. Why couldn't Trace have——' He broke off, then, 'Well, I'll just have to think of something else.'

Gwen knitted her brows. 'What do you mean?'

'Hmm? Oh, just that I—er—will have a word with Trace about you.'

'No, Leo,' she said forcefully, 'please don't interfere. I know you mean well, but——'

A masculine hand reached over her shoulder to take the phone from her. '—but we'll thank you to keep your nose out of our marriage,' Brad said into the mouthpiece, and hung up.

'*Do you mind?*' Gwen said freezingly. 'I was having a private conversation with my godfather and wasn't ready to end it yet.'

'What was he doing on the phone to you at this time of the night?' asked Brad.

'Saying goodbye. He's flying to New York tonight.'

'Good riddance!' he growled.

'You haven't even met him, Bradley, so why are you talking like that?'

'Frustration, Gwen. Pure frustration.'

With grim intent, Brad pulled her to him. One hand raked through her hair, the other caught her chin in a relentless vice, and then he was kissing her—deeply, thoroughly, hungrily. Gwen was shocked motionless for the space of several seconds by this sudden, shattering possession of her mouth in a manner so intimate and familiar that it was as if he'd done it before. And off that thought ricocheted a memory that yanked her out of Brad's arms in stunned disbelief.

'You did kiss me that night,' she whispered, touching

trembling fingers to her throbbing mouth. 'It wasn't a dream, either.'

'And you kissed me back. *Boy*, did you kiss me back!' He drew her to him. 'Do it again,' he ordered softly, and lowered his head to prompt her along.

'Bradley.' Gwen tried to pull away from the drugging exploration of his lips. She couldn't believe she'd forgotten such an eventful episode in their relationship. 'Why didn't you tell me?'

'Oh, sure. Just walk right up to you and say, "Gwen, you beautiful idiot, you obviously don't remember, but we had a pretty hot time of it Friday night when you got home, and came damn close to going to bed together."'

'We did not!' she exclaimed.

Brad raised his head to show her a mocking smile. 'Well, you had my robe untied, and I call that pretty close.' She blushed furiously and a wicked gleam appeared in his eyes. 'Now you remember, don't you?'

'No, I don't,' Gwen denied, but she was lying. She remembered it all now. Vividly and in great detail.

'Perhaps this will help remind you.'

This time his kiss was restrained, nibbling at her lips with soft persuasion. It succeeded very nicely in melting every bone in Gwen's body. All resistance gone, she reached up and entangled her fingers in his hair, drawing his head down further to increase the pressure of his mouth on hers. Brad's hold tightened and he slid a hand caressingly down her back to mould her slim length hard against his. Gwen made a yearning sound in her throat, wanting more. She wrapped her arms around his neck and gave herself up to the mouth plundering, devouring hers, and when it seemed about to lift she stretched to capture it again. Every feeling, every memory of Friday night in the kitchen was flooding through her, adding to the passion now taking control of her body. She was helpless in its clutching grip, possessed by an aching need to assuage it.

Her hand slid around to fumble with the shirt button at Brad's throat, slipped inside his collar to caress the warm skin beneath. She dragged her mouth from his and kissed a wandering line to his shoulder, pushing his collar aside in order to probe further. *This* was what she wanted. To be able at last to give in to her longing to touch Brad and have him touch her. To smell his flagrantly masculine skin up close. To feel the strength of his male body beneath her roaming hands. To know that a bright new future was opening up for her, a future that could include love as well as a career. After convincing herself that such a life was impossible and not to be remotely thought of, the wonder of discovering that she would be sharing this perfect dream with Brad brought a rush of relief and happiness. She arched back in his arms to look at him, a smile of love in her eyes and teasing words on her lips.

'Gwen, come to bed with me.'

Brad whispered the request, his heated gaze on her mouth, his hand moving to cup her breast through the material of her T-shirt. Gwen froze, not believing what she'd just heard. But the next instant her body was reacting to what her mind tried to deny. The smile shattered in her eyes, the words died unspoken on her lips. She wrenched herself away from him with such force that she stumbled several steps backward into one of the high counter stools. It wobbled against the one beside it and both toppled over with a loud clatter of wood.

Gwen could only stare at Brad, temporarily bereft of all speech and feeling, then, with a small, choked cry, she bolted past him and ran to her room, banging the door shut behind her and leaning against it as she raised shaking hands to her face. Brad wanted sex, not love. *Sex.* There was no bright future ahead of them, only the selfish immediacy of his lust.

The doorknob turned and pressure was applied to the door. 'Gwen, let me in! We have to talk.'

Furious with herself for being such a damned naïve fool and just as furious at Brad for playing so carelessly with her vulnerable feelings, Gwen stepped back and threw the door wide. The hurt would come later, she knew. Right now she had to pretend that his kisses hadn't meant a thing to her.

'I'm so sorry, Bradley,' she apologised with all the sarcasm she could muster, 'I left before you could finish the job of seducing me. That was your intention, wasn't it?'

'I didn't notice you objecting,' he gritted out, not moving from the doorway. 'And it's a moot point who was seducing whom.'

'You've been working up to that all week!' she stormed, seeing it clearly now. 'Thursday evening when Corinne Mason was here and last night at the restaurant are just two instances of your—your *flirting*, to give your tricks a polite term. And you're the one who said there'd be no involvement between us!'

'By involvement I take it you mean sex?'

'I thought we were *friends*, Bradley.' It was a cry of disillusionment that he didn't seem to hear.

'I don't want to be your friend, Gwen.' He jerked her to him. 'I want to be your lover.'

She twisted out of his grasp. Hearing him state his intentions so bluntly killed a quivering shred of hope that she had put too hasty an interpretation on his invitation to go to bed with him. Cold wrath overwhelmed the threat of tears and she sought words to hurt him as he had hurt her. 'I don't *want* a lover, thank you very much! I don't want a husband, either, but since I've got one I would greatly appreciate it if he would stop mauling me about.'

'All work and no play is bad for the brain.' Brad let his gaze travel insolently down her length. 'Not to mention that delectable body of yours.'

'Allow me to know what's best for my brain, *and* my body,' Gwen shot back. 'Sex with you is not best. In fact it's at the bottom of my list of priorities. I find my studies hold a far greater fascination for me. You, although your charms are tempting, I must admit, can't even begin to compare.'

'We're really getting nasty now, aren't we?' mocked Brad. 'Does this mean we're no longer friends?'

'If it does, that's fine with me,' she snapped.

'Have it your way, then. Good night.'

'*Good night.*'

Their chilly parting was the beginning of a mutual freeze that manifested itself in scrupulous avoidance of each other over the next week.

Their bitter confrontation had left Gwen deeply upset, and it wasn't until Friday that her wounded feelings began to accept the salve of reasoned thinking. Instead of pinning all the blame on her allegedly selfish and heartless husband, she started to pin half of it on herself. She had been drawn to Brad almost from the beginning, and no matter how strenuously she had tried to put her studies ahead of that attraction, she'd always known deep down inside that it was simply biding its time. And when he'd kissed her, she'd given in to what she felt, both on the night of her birthday and last Sunday night. It wasn't Brad's fault that she'd tried to place in his heart what was in her own. Just because she cared about him it didn't mean he felt the same way about her, and thinking so had been far too presumptuous. He liked her, certainly. He would no doubt enjoy a physical liaison with her because of that liking. But his love wouldn't enter into the relationship, and Gwen couldn't force it to. Should she judge him guilty because of it? Or should she accept his behaviour for what it really was—that of a man who found her attractive and had been encouraged by her response to his kisses to assume that she would welcome an interlude in bed with him?

It took most of her Friday classes to help Gwen put the situation in perspective, but she still retained some of her anger at Brad, despite shouldering her share of the blame for their fight. He should have contained his physical desires just as she had, taking the same care not to jeopardise the delicate balance of their living arrangement, especially as there were still eleven long months to go of their so-called marriage. Now, having experienced each other's passion, they were stuck with frustrated hungers that would have to live unsatisfied and a constraint that was going to make life difficult. The more Gwen thought about it, the more blame she shifted right back to Brad's side of the fence. After all, he had made the first move, causing her to forget all the

promises she had made to herself to keep their
relationship friendly and non-romantic. And his motive
for making that move had been totally self-serving,
having everything to do with sex and nothing to do
with making love. There was a great difference between
the two, in Gwen's mind. At least she had kissed him
with something close to love, whereas he ... He had
kissed her with the idea of making her his lover, and
love and caring had never entered his heart, let alone
his thick skull. Stupid man!

Gwen was still feeling somewhat righteous when she
received an unexpected phone call from her godfather
on Friday morning after Brad had left for work. It was
seven-thirty; ten-thirty in New York. Leo said he'd
wanted to catch her before she left for her classes.

'You're lucky,' she responded. 'I was just on my way
out the door. How are you, Leo?'

'Keeping busy. And you?'

'Same here. Studying hard, as usual.'

'Have—er—you and Brad sorted out your differences?'

Gwen wondered briefly at the note of hopefulness in
her godfather's voice, but as his question addressed
itself to, at present, her least favourite subject, she didn't
dwell on it. 'On the contrary,' she said, 'we've
progressed and are now at each other's throats. Or
were. Currently, we're barely speaking to each other.
Next comes the divorce.'

'Divorce?' Leo echoed in consternation.

'Not really. I still need Brad's money and he still
needs me as a wife.' Gwen shot a look at the kitchen
clock. 'I'm sorry, Leo, but I have to run or I'll be late.
Thanks for calling. It's always good to hear from you.'

'Gwen, wait. Do you—like Brad at all?'

'Ha!' was all she said, which said plenty, none of it
accurate.

Leo persisted, 'Well, he's nice, isn't he?'

'He's an insufferable know-it-all who puts his own
interpretation on whatever I say or do and expects me
to fall in with it, that's what he is. Among other things
just as bad. Leo, I really do have to go. Can I call you
tonight?'

'I'm off to Japan this afternoon.' He tried for some encouragement. 'When I return next month, maybe you and Brad will have made up.'

'Not a chance,' Gwen said uncompromisingly. 'We're both satisfied with the way things are now. Goodbye, Leo. Talk to you next month.'

She hung up and made her usual dash for the bus. Her thoughts were tied up neatly with no room for adjustment: Brad was out for fun and games, she had merely reacted to the expert kisses of a man she happened to like, he had tried to take unfair advantage of that lapse, and she, having momentarily lost all common sense, had very nearly let him. It was as simple as that. She now had her common sense back, Brad was undoubtedly finding what he wanted with Corinne, and he and Gwen had once more returned to the pursuit of their separate lives with no worry that the other would hinder them in any way. In fact, they had become strangers, and what did strangers care about each other? Nothing. Which suited her just fine.

It was while entering the local liquor store that afternoon that Gwen ran smack into the person whom she cared nothing about.

'Bradley——!' she exclaimed.

His hand steadied her. 'What are you doing here?' he frowned.

'Shopping. Why aren't you at your office?'

'I left early. Here, give me that.' He took the load of groceries from her arms. 'Did you want something in there?' His brief nod indicated the liquor store.

'Yes, a bottle of wine. I——'

'There's wine at home.' He placed his own purchase in the shopping bag and grasped her arm with hard fingers. 'Come on, I'll drive you there.'

'You're hurting me,' Gwen objected.

His grip relaxed slightly. 'Planning a cosy party, are you?'

'A cosy——?'

'Well, you can't have it at the apartment. I have guests waiting there, so you and your group will have to party elsewhere.' He unlocked the front passenger door of his car and almost pushed her inside.

'But I——' The door slammed in Gwen's face. 'Well, really!' It was easy to see that, unlike her own, Brad's temper had not improved with the passage of days. She twisted around to face him as he slid into his own seat. 'What in heaven's name are you mad about now?' she demanded.

'Fasten your seatbelt,' he ordered.

'Answer me, Bradley!'

'I'm not mad. This is my natural state since you moved in.' He shoved the paper shopping bag at her. 'Hang on to this. I can't drive with it in my lap.'

Gwen made a grab for it as the car shot forward. 'Bradley, slow down!'

'Have you invited your boy-friend to the party?'

'What party? Bradley, I said slow down! You can get yourself into an accident, but not me with you.'

His foot eased off the accelerator a bit and Gwen sat back in relief. Brad was looking slightly gaunt. Hadn't he been eating, for heaven's sake? 'Why aren't you with your guests if they're already at the apartment?' she wanted to know.

'We ran out of Scotch. Don't you bother checking the stock?'

'If you wouldn't drink so much of it you wouldn't go through it so fast,' Gwen pointed out.

His expression blackened. 'You don't like my driving, you don't like my drinking—is there anything else you'd care to mention while you're at it?'

'Yes, your smoking in the den,' she answered promptly. 'You've been doing it all week and it smells up the whole room.'

'It needed only that,' he said grimly.

'Well, it does. I thought we had an agreement, Bradley.'

'I have no intention of changing my habits—bad or otherwise—for any whim of yours, Gwen.'

'There's no otherwise about it,' she told him roundly. 'All your habits are bad. You're rude, nasty——'

'Those aren't habits, they're traits,' Brad corrected. 'And spare me the rest of your homily, Gwen. I'm not in the mood to listen to it.'

Her mouth closed with a snap and she sat in fuming silence for the remainder of the drive home. What had ever made her think that there was anything to like about Brad? There was nothing to like about him. Zero. Zilch. He was a one hundred per cent pain in the neck, and why the hell hadn't he been eating?

Brad stopped her as she unlocked the door to their corner suite.

'Keep a lid on that temper of yours and don't go insulting my guests,' he ordered.

'*My* temper! Of all the . . .!' Gwen drew a deep breath and pinned a smile on her face. 'I won't say one nasty word,' she promised sweetly.

'See that you don't,' he warned, unimpressed.

She yanked the bag of groceries from him and pushed open the door. Brad went straight down to the living-room, taking the bottle of Scotch with him. Gwen heard Corinne greet him languidly.

'That's all I need!' she muttered, slamming the bag down on the kitchen counter. She began putting food away with careless abandon. Corinne's voice floated up to her from below the open-sided dining-room opposite the kitchen.

'Oh, go on, Brad, invite her to join us for a moment. She can have a drink with us if she likes. Or is she allowed to drink yet? A student, isn't she? Well, maybe just a sip, then.'

That was too much for Gwen to take passively. She was not a child to be given gracious permission to join the adults for half an hour of amusing entertainment. This was her home and she'd better establish her territorial rights immediately. She smoothed her hair, the light of battle in her eyes, and walked sedately downstairs to the living-room. There were only two guests.

'Excuse me,' she said tentatively. 'I have to get the sewing basket. Don't let me interrupt you, though.'

Brad was sitting in one of the armchairs beside the fireplace, his long legs stretched out before him. At her words, he looked up sharply, his eyes narrowing in hard suspicion. 'The sewing basket is in the hall cupboard.'

'Oh.' Gwen frowned in apparent thought. 'Are you sure? I used it this morning to sew a missing button on one of your shirts.'

His mouth tightened, but before he could speak Shane Michaels was there to draw her forward.

'Perhaps you could delay your sewing for a while to join us,' he suggested gravely, but there was a twinkle in his eyes.

'Thank you, but I wouldn't dream of intruding,' she demurred prettily.

Brad's suspicion increased tenfold. Gwen at her most innocent was Gwen looking for trouble. He watched her with suddenly wary attention.

'You wouldn't be intruding at all,' Shane was saying. 'We're having a meeting away from the demands of Brad's office and would welcome a break.'

'Well, I wouldn't mind socialising a bit.' She smiled at him. 'Being a wife keeps me so busy!'

Corinne spoke up lazily. 'When it comes right down to it, you're not Brad's wife, are you?'

'No, no, I'm just pretending. Aren't I, Bradley?' Gwen sat down primly on the couch.

'Don't you have a class to go to or something?' he asked irritably, reaching for his cigarettes.

'I'm playing hooky. School's so boring. Do you suppose I could have a sip of sherry if I promise not to dance on the furniture?'

His lighter flicked shut with something of a snap.

'I'm certain Brad has no objection to your having any kind of drink you like,' Shane assured her on a note of underlying laughter. 'Sweet or dry?'

'Sweet, please.'

'So.' Corinne leaned back in her chair and crossed one shapely leg over the other, examining Gwen in a manner meant to discomfit her. 'Are you a good pretend wife to Brad? Cook his meals, iron his shirts, make his bed?'

'Oh, yes, I do everything like that,' Gwen responded chattily. 'All the housework, the cooking, laundry, *every*thing. I do think a man should have someone to look after those little things for him, don't you?' She accepted a glass of sherry from Shane. 'Thank you. Mmm, this is very good, Bradley.'

'You should be a judge,' he observed sardonically, even while noting how lovely she looked in a turquoise jumpsuit tightly cinched in at the waist by a wide black leather belt. That had been his problem ever since his return from Toronto two weeks ago—being aware of Gwen's every expression and gesture, her bright vitality, her damnably persistent habit of attracting him to everything she did. Even this tall tale she was telling only entwined him further around her little finger. The cheeky little liar! Well he remembered her stinging comments about pulling his own weight in the matter of household chores. He remembered everything, including sharing some passionate kisses that had been over far too soon, and sharp words that should never have been spoken. If only . . . Corinne's rather grating voice broke in on Brad's moody thoughts.

'A young girl like you must find it a trifle embarrassing to deal with things like a man's laundry,' she pursued.

'A trifle,' Gwen agreed, 'but I close my eyes when handling the more personal items, so it's not too bad.'

Shane choked on his Martini and she looked at him in surprise, conveying the impression that she had been perfectly sincere and didn't understand his amusement.

Corinne's eyes narrowed. 'How old are you, anyway? Eighteen or thereabouts?'

'Actually, I'm only sixteen, but I'm well developed for my age. That's probably what fooled you into thinking I was older.'

'Gwen . . .' Brad began warningly.

'That's all right, darling,' Corinne trilled. 'She's obviously touchy about it.'

He rose to refill his glass, saying shortly, 'She's twenty-one years old and not touchy at all.' *And stop calling me darling*, he thought savagely. *I'm already in enough hot water with my wife. I don't need you making bad into worse.*

Brad was beginning to wish he hadn't brought Corinne home with him. But he'd known that Gwen

finished classes early on Fridays, and he'd hoped that
the other woman might provoke a little jealousy in her.
So far, though, not a sign of it had transpired. Gwen
seemed more intent on baiting him through Corinne.
Hell, hadn't she had her fill of fighting? He knew he
had. All he wanted now was to kiss and make up.

'Would you care to stay to dinner?' Gwen asked
Shane in her best hostess manner. 'And you too, of
course, Corinne. Or has Brad been ahead of me with
the invitation?'

'We're dining out,' Brad said curtly, pouring his
drink.

'I'm sorry to hear that.' She gave a heartrending sigh.
'Another evening, perhaps.' Brad's head turned and his
blue eyes raked Gwen with a look that made her small
chin jut out. 'Where are you going to eat?' she enquired
politely of Shane. 'Someplace fancy?'

'To the Mansion. We'd be happy to have you join us,
wouldn't we, Brad?'

He raised his glass and said coolly, 'Gwen has several
chores she wants to get done this evening.' Malice
tinged his voice. 'Several of those *little things* she enjoys
doing for me so much.'

'It's true,' she said regretfully. 'I have to darn his
socks next.' She shook her head in mock sorrow. 'A
woman's work is never done!'

'Perhaps you'd like to get started on your "woman's
work" right now,' hinted Brad. Two could play at this
game!

Gwen turned her shoulder on him. 'So the three of
you are going to the Mansion, are you? I hope you
don't intend to go in Brad's car.'

'Oh? Why is that?' Shane shot a brimming look at his
friend's stiffening form.

'Well, I don't mean to criticise my husband's driving,'
she said untruthfully, 'but don't you think you'd be
taking your life in your hands?'

'You think so?' Shane appeared to seriously consider
the matter, ignoring the incensed look he received from
Brad.

'Yes. I mean, it's bad enough that Bradley risks his

own life, but those of his friends?' Gwen clicked her
tongue in disapproval and leaned forward to set her
glass on the coffee table.

'His name's Brad,' snapped Corinne.

'I beg your pardon?'

A glittering smile touched the older woman's thin
lips. 'He detests being called Bradley, didn't anyone tell
you?'

'No, they didn't,' Gwen replied lightly. 'How remiss
of them!'

'I'm surprised Brad hasn't told you himself. But
perhaps he didn't want to hurt your feelings.'

'I don't think that could be the reason.' Gwen
directed a look of enquiry at him. 'Was that the reason,
darling?'

Annoyance crossed Brad's face. Damn that Corinne!
Bringing her here had been definitely bad strategy; she
didn't faze Gwen a bit. He picked up his glass with a
jerk, spilling some of the contents on to the bar, and
Gwen jumped up with alacrity.

'Let me wipe that up for you, honeybunch.' She
produced a cloth from below. 'You're so sloppy,
sweetie pie,' she scolded, wiping the spot dry. 'I'm
always cleaning up after you.'

'You're asking for it, Gwen,' he muttered savagely
under his breath.

She displayed hurt surprise. 'Don't get mad at me,
lambchop. You're the one who was careless.'

'That's right, Brad,' Shane chipped in. 'Blame
yourself, not your poor wife.' He was containing his
laughter, but just barely. It was plain that he was
enjoying the whole situation.

Corinne, however, was not. 'Let's go, Brad,' she
commanded, rising to her feet. 'I find the sugary
atmosphere around here sickening.'

Gwen was immediately concerned. 'Maybe you
should lie down. Corinne. Can I get you anything?
Aspirin, perhaps? Or how about a nice glass of warm
milk?'

This proved to be too much for Shane's control. His
laugh rang out in pure delight and he stood up to hug

Gwen briefly to him. 'My God, you're a priceless treasure! I think you'd better keep your wife, Brad, because if you don't, I will.'

Brad banged his glass down. That did it! He yanked Gwen from the other's casual embrace with a force that whipped her head back and slammed her against the solid wall of his chest. 'Excuse us,' he said tightly to an amused Shane and a self-satisfied Corinne.

She probably thinks he's going to turn me over his knee and give me a good spanking, Gwen thought wildly as she was dragged from the living-room by the wrist. One look at Brad's face told her that possibility was not all that far-fetched. Just let him try, she vowed, knowing she'd been playing with fire and ready to start a whole inferno if that was what he wanted.

Brad swung her into her room and kicked the door shut behind him. She faced him with blustering challenge and a certain amount of secondary caution. His mouth twitched involuntarily. Then a reluctant smile tugged at one corner and his shoulders began to shake. He was laughing!

Gwen was not reassured. 'I don't like being treated like that by Corinne, Bradley.'

'So I gathered.' He crossed the room to flop down into an armchair by the window, still gripped by low laughter. She'd won, the vixen! How could he resist her? 'You're a wretch, Gwen, do you know that? Poor Corinne, I swear she thinks I'm going to punish you for talking to her as you did.'

'Fom the expression on your face when you dragged me away, what else would she think?'

'I *should* punish you,' he said. 'Put you on bread and water, at the very least. Fortunately, however, you haven't yet succeeded in ridding me of what little sense of humour I have left.'

'I wasn't aware that you had *any*.' Gwen sat down on her bed, rubbing her sore wrist. Like a splash of cold water on burning coals, the bad feeling between them had been abruptly doused. But the taint of it was still present. She looked at him unhappily. 'Why were you mad at me in the first place, Bradley?'

'I wasn't mad.' He rose and came to sit down beside her, taking her wrist in his hands. 'I was merely—disappointed. Did I hurt you?'

'No. Disappointed about what?'

'You'd left an opened letter from your friend Kelly on the kitchen table. I caught a glimpse of one line when I placed it on top of the fridge. She was asking you to spend this Thanksgiving weekend with her in Victoria.'

'Don't you want me to?' Gwen asked hopefully.

'You can do as you please. It's just that I don't have any plans for the holiday, and I'm going to be awfully lonely here all by myself.' Brad sighed loudly, playing it for all it was worth.

She pushed scoffingly at his shoulder with her free hand. 'What a sob story! You just want me to stay around and cook a big turkey dinner for you.'

'No, I'll do the cooking, but I need you to do the dishes afterwards,' he explained.

'That figures.' Gwen watched for a moment as his fingers continued to smooth the slightly reddened skin on her wrist. 'That letter is a few days old, Bradley, and I've already told Kelly that I can't make it over there this weekend. I was just having second thoughts this morning, because I didn't know what you'd be doing, what with our fight and all.'

'I'm spending it with my roommate. And that fight is now officially over. Agreed?'

She hesitated. 'Yes, it's over, but there is a matter that has yet to be resolved.'

'How do you want to resolve it?' he asked quietly.

Gwen stood up jerkily, folding her arms across her stomach as she took a couple of agitated steps away from him. He was leaving the direction of their relationship up to her, and she knew what she had to say. It wasn't what she wanted, but what was best—for both of them.

'We have eleven more months to go of this marriage, Bradley.'

'I know.'

She turned to face him, trying to speak around the

lump in her throat. 'Everything was fine until we . . .
until you——' She broke off, unable to explain in a few
words all that had happened to her in those moments of
kissing.

'Until I kissed you,' Brad supplied flatly.

'I think it would be better if we remained just
friends,' Gwen said in a rush.

'You're really stuck on this friendship kick, aren't
you?'

She looked straight at him. 'Would you rather we be
enemies?'

'No. I don't think I could bear that.' Brad came to
stand in front of her. 'All right—friends. Maybe once
we get to know each other better we can become
something more.' He tipped her head back and kissed
her on the mouth. 'That was merely a friendly kiss.
Nothing more intended.'

'Good,' Gwen said lightly, struggling to hide the
effect the touch of his mouth had on her, 'because that's
all we are, or ever will be.'

Brad studied her face thoughtfully, then smiled.
'We'll see.'

No, we won't, she thought. It hurt to reject even the
temporary intimacy he was offering, but she had to do
it. She was teetering on the edge of love as it was.
Becoming lovers with him would push her over, and
eventually she would hit flat bottom, with a long hard
climb to emotional recovery. And, in the end, she would
still be alone, Brad's exit from her life as guaranteed as
the one-year contract they had signed. So it was better
to move far back from the precipice, and not fall at all.
Better, but just as painful.

Striving to speak normally, Gwen voiced a question
that had been niggling at the back of her mind. 'Do you
really dislike being called by your full name, Bradley?'

His face chilled. 'My grandfather always addressed
me like that. Even after all this time, I still find it an
unpleasant reminder.'

'You should have told me.'

His expression softened, his hand coming up to
smooth a swatch of raven-silk hair behind her ear. 'The

way you say it makes everything better, Gwen. Don't ever stop.'

'What did he do to you that was so bad?' she asked, yearning to take away some of the hurt she could sense in him.

'He betrayed me.' Brad's hand fell away, his mouth hardening at memories he wouldn't share. 'What time does your party start?'

Gwen frowned in puzzlement. 'You keep harping on a party. *What* party?'

'Open house, remember? It *is* Friday.'

'Oh, that. Bradley, I only said that because I was mad. I don't want an advance on my allowance.'

He was watching her out of suddenly distant eyes. 'But you do want money.'

'I don't *want* it. I *need* it.' Gwen couldn't tell him why. She'd seen Brad's ruthless side, and even knowing him as well as she did now, she was unconsciously wary of giving him a weapon. And her beloved family, used against her, would be a very effective weapon should Brad for some reason take it in mind to make her love, honour and obey. The time would come to tell him— when trust did. She slipped her hand into his in a gesture of entreaty. 'That's different, Bradley—very different. Will you believe that?'

'Yes, I'll believe it.' He didn't want to do otherwise, because otherwise was too disturbing to think about. Hunger for all the things Gwen wouldn't give him burned inside him. 'Come to dinner with us,' he invited, his fingers tightening around hers.

'I can't. There's an essay I have to work on, and a textbook I——'

'I get the picture,' he said abruptly, releasing her hand. 'I'll be home late. Don't wait up for me.'

'I won't, Bradley,' Gwen replied, watching him head for the bedroom door. She'd learned her lesson—he'd have her as a lover, but not as a real wife. She wouldn't wait. For anything.

CHAPTER SEVEN

THE decline of Brad's and Gwen's relationship started the day after their mutual understanding had been reached. At first it wasn't apparent. Brad stopped smoking entirely, stopped all but the occasional social drinking, seemingly falling in with Gwen's strictures on his habits. In truth, the life had gone out of him. He got up, went to work, came back. Nothing interested him. He didn't smile, but neither did he frown. The high polish that usually stamped his work disappeared. Things that he had once thought important—his company, money, self-reliance—hardly mattered any more. The world had gone grey, blotting out all the sunshine. And the one person who could bring back the colours was too damned busy cramming her way to a university degree.

October drifted into November, and never for a moment was Gwen unaware of the slow but definite change occurring in the way she and Brade treated each other. They performed their allotted chores silently and quickly, with none of the friendly swapping of insults that had marked earlier days. Their conversations centred on impersonal subjects. The politeness of strangers crept into their daily encounters. It was all a gradual development that each couldn't help notice but which neither spoke of, and the reason for it was the same for both. Too much had happened to let them be satisfied with friendship, and the strain of trying to pretend they could be was greater than they could handle.

On a Monday morning in mid-November, five weeks into this new state of affairs, Gwen went into the kitchen after her swim to find Brad already dressed and at the stove cooking breakfast. She said a quiet good morning, thinking as she often did how dearly familiar he was, with his golden hair still drying from

his shower and his athletic body clad in a crisp dress shirt
and co-ordinated slacks. The jacket half of his business
suit was always fitted over the back of a kitchen chair
until he was ready to leave. Passing it now, Gwen
paused to lightly brush her fingers over its collar. It had
been so long since she had touched Brad—so terribly,
terribly long. And not just physically, but mentally, too.
The spark that had always enlivened their up-and-down
relationship was missing. Now they were just acquaint-
ances, sharing nothing but the space around them.

'I'm flying to Calgary this morning,' he told her.

Gwen stared at Brad's back with a stricken expression.
He was transferring eggs and bacon from the frying pan
to two plates, and hadn't even glanced around when
he'd dropped his bombshell. 'How ... how long will
you be gone?'

'All week. I hope no more than that.'

She sat down slowly at the kitchen table. A whole
week! She couldn't bear it. To be alone again, without
him. Their behaviour of late hadn't been anything to
treasure, but still, Brad had been here with her, if not in
the same room, then somewhere else in the apartment.

'Eat your breakfast, Gwen,' he said, setting a plate
before her.

'I'm not hungry,' she whispered.

Brad's eyes were steady on her. 'Will you be all right
here while I'm gone?'

'Why should you be concerned?' she asked, her voice
catching. 'You weren't when you left me alone for the
first two weeks of our marriage.'

'Gwen——'

Pushing back her chair, she stumbled to her feet.
'Excuse me, I'm going to be late for class. Have a nice
trip, Bradley.'

He had already left for his office when Gwen came
out of her room twenty minutes later. He was in
Calgary when she returned to the apartment that
evening. She curled up on the couch with two
affectionate kittens in her arms and stared at the ceiling,
eventually drifting off to sleep as night fell. She awoke
in the cold dawn, shivering, and went upstairs to crawl

into bed, clothes and all. She didn't go to her Tuesday classes. She didn't do anything on Tuesday, feeling as if she had lost something she would never find again. She forced herself to attend classes on Wednesday and Thursday. Friday was a lost cause as she waited desperately for the sound of Brad's key in the lock. Shane phoned each evening to see how she was. She was fine, she told him. Brad never called once.

If his absence did nothing else for her, it showed Gwen that she loved Brad. Totally, Completely. For ever. Her thoughts were filled with him, nearly every waking moment concerned with his safety, whether he was eating his three square meals a day, worry that he was working himself too hard again.   It was a period of heavy introspection for Gwen. She wanted Brad, and she wanted her career. Convinced that she couldn't have both, she weighed the pros and cons of each, agonising over which to choose. She thought of the financial security she would have for both herself and her family if she continued on her climb to a corporate career, with no delaying stops on the way. And she thought incessantly of what she could have with Brad, even for a little while, if she accepted an intimate relationship with him. Her imagination conjured up delights, but also caused torment. What if something happened to him on this trip to Calgary? She would never know the possession of his body, would never discover whether he actually loved her as she sometimes suspected.

Perhaps it was the knowledge that she would always regret not sharing a real marriage with Brad, for however short a time, that helped Gwen make the decision. Whatever it was, her heart, after a long, upsetting battle, finally took over from her mind. Brad was her security—not financially, but through the warmth of his smile and the strength of his caring. He made her happy, gave her the base from which she could go on to a better future. Without him, she would find success and financial stability, but she would lose the spirit that made her special to herself, to Brad, and to others. And everyone would be losers in the end.

Money could be found, worked at, saved. But the spirit, when gone, was gone for ever. She couldn't sacrifice that for a career, for it was all she would have left should everything else disappear.

A certain serenity came over Gwen upon reaching this new level of self-awareness, and she did the one thing she had sworn to herself six weeks ago she'd never do—she waited. For the week to pass, for Brad to come home, for her love to be consummated with as much of him as he was willing to give her. And if he couldn't return her love, then their marriage would end in nine and a half months with no bitterness, no regret. *She* would love *him*, and be happier for it, even if sadness followed.

Brad arrived back on Saturday evening. Gwen came out of her room dressed for bed to find him already at the top of the stairs leading down to the living-room. He was in the grey suit he had been wearing the day they first met, and looked so tired and alone that she felt everything her heart had to offer reaching out to him.

'Bradley!' His name left Gwen's lips involuntarily, all her pent-up need in that one word. He turned sharply and suddenly she was across the intervening space and in his arms. 'I've missed you so much, Bradley,' she whispered, clinging to him tightly, her ribs threatening to crack in his own crushing hug. 'Please don't leave me again. Don't . . .'

His mouth closed over the last word without gentleness. Gwen strained her body against his, fiercely seeking her own pleasure from the savage kiss that was whipping the hot blood of desire into their bodies. Their mouths strained together, hungry for intimate contact. Their hands searched and found and caressed with rough urgency. They were man and woman, heading rapidly, finally, towards their ultimate goal.

Carried away by the unleashed power of their passion, neither was aware of exactly how things happened. Somehow they were in Gwen's room. Somehow they were on the wide double bed, their roused bodies naked and wanting. Gwen clutched Brad to her, entangling her legs with his, trying to hold back a moan as his tongue swirled across her taut nipple. He moved his mouth to her other breast and gently suckled it, causing a million sensations to shoot through her fully awakened body. She pulled his head up, hungry for more of his kisses.

Brad stopped holding back in expectancy of her retreat. His mouth roughened on hers, seeking and finding a passionate response. His fingers stroked her, teasing, arousing, and Gwen whimpered, a tiny sound. There was no going back. Brad was opening a whole new world to her and she had to experience it totally, not just this tantalising glimpse of it. She responded without thought, with only love and desire and an age-old urge to become one with Brad.

'You win, Bradley,' she murmured against the searing heat of his mouth. 'We'll be lovers for as long as you want.'

Every muscle in his body froze, then he was grabbing her hands and whipping them up above her head. 'What the hell do you mean—I win?' he snarled, looking down at her with blazing eyes.

Confusion held Gwen immobile. 'You said you—isn't this what you wanted?'

He cursed and sat up, swinging his legs to the floor. 'I'm not looking for a sacrifice, Gwen,' he snapped, reaching for his trousers and pulling them on.

'Bradley, I want it, too!' she cried, sitting up with him.

'You don't know *what* you want.'

'Yes, I do.' But he was already on his way out of the room and didn't hear her response. 'Yes, I do know what I want,' Gwen repeated softly, tearfully to herself. 'You just won't let me give it to you.' She drew the bedcovers up around her shivering form. 'I love you, Bradley. I love you so much.'

It took several rings before the noise of the phone finally intruded on Gwen's misery. She pulled on a robe and unwillingly went to pick up the kitchen extension.

'Hello, Gwen, it's Leo. I'm in Los Angeles and thought I'd give you a call. How are you?'

'I—Leo, I'd rather not talk right now, okay? I've just had a—an argument . . . with Brad and it's left me a little upset. Could I call you tomorrow?'

'*Another* fight?' asked Leo, dismayed.

'We're always fighting,' Gwen said listlessly. 'I'll call you tomorrow, Leo. Goodbye.'

She hung up, forgetting that she didn't have the number where he was staying. The apartment was silent. Brad had gone out again. Gwen returned to her room and discarded her robe to draw on a concealing, floor-length flannel nightgown. Brad's shirt, tie and jacket were still lying on the carpet where they had been tossed. Gwen turned away from them and got into the cold side of her bed, her head throbbing.

Two hours later she was still wide awake, her headache increasing its grip of pain. She stuck it out for another hour, then reluctantly slid out of bed and stumbled into the bathroom for a pain-killer. Then she walked carefully to the kitchen, where she boiled some milk. Maybe that would ease her into sleep. But when she closed her bedroom door she froze in mid-step as her gaze fell on the surprise awaiting her. 'Bradley!' she exclaimed, shocked. 'What are you doing in my bed?'

'Sleeping.' He was stretched out on his stomach, his head cradled in his arms. 'Don't pick another fight with me tonight, Gwen,' he said, not opening his eyes. 'All I want to do is sleep.'

She was immediately indignant. '*I* don't pick fights with you—*you* pick fights with *me.*"

'What are you doing now, then?'

'I'm just telling you——' Gwen broke off in frustration. Her gaze jerked down Brad's naked back to the point just above his hips where the covers began. Was he *wearing* anything beneath the blankets? She squared her shoulders determinedly. 'Now listen, Bradley, you can't sleep here and that's all there is to it.' Especially since you rejected me and my bed when offered to you earlier, she thought grimly.

No answer. Gwen marched across the room and picked up a barrette from the nightstand to poke him in the shoulder. He rolled on to his side in sleepy annoyance.

'What the hell was that?'

'Bradley, get out of my bed!'

He collapsed on to the pillow again. 'I'm not going to do anything but sleep, Gwen—for now. Your virtue is still safe.'

Gwen flung around and almost tripped over his clothes on the floor. She picked up the discarded items and shook them out. 'You don't have very tidy habits,' she criticised, draping them over a straight-backed chair. She turned around again and looked longingly at her pillow. 'If I let you stay, will you promise to keep on your own side?'

'I promise,' he mumbled.

His answer did not please Gwen. Muttering to herself, she cautiously slipped in beside him, smoothing her long nightgown around her ankles before lying down. When Brad didn't move, she switched off the lamp with an irritated click. Here she was just where he'd wanted her, and all he could do was *sleep*!

'Don't fall off the bed.' His voice, drowsy and amused, rippled over her in the dark.

'Why should I?' she snapped.

'You're so close to the edge of it, I'm afraid you might.'

She suppressed an urge to kick his shin. 'You're enjoying this, aren't you?'

'Yes, I am. It's a very comfortable bed. Good night.'

Gwen's frustration broke free. '*Don't* you tell me good night, Bradley Robilliard!' she burst out, grabbing her pillow and thumping him across the stomach with it.

He tore it from her grasp and rolled on top of her, his long, heavy body pinning her slim form to the mattress. 'Something bothering you, Gwen?' he asked with a soft chuckle, his night-darkened head mere inches above hers.

She accepted his weight with warm satisfaction, her hands going immediately to the sides of his waist. He had only his shorts on, and she lovingly stroked the bare skin above the waistband. 'I don't want my virtue to be safe, Bradley,' she whispered in the darkness. 'Nor do I want to be a sacrifice. I just want us to make love.'

'So do I.'

'Then why did you leave me earlier?' Gwen hadn't understood it then, and the hurt in her voice told him she didn't understand it now.

Brad's big hand cupped the back of her head. 'We both need to go into this with our eyes wide open, Gwen. It might not last.'

She was silent. He'd said out loud what she'd only thought, but included a qualifier she'd been too scared to consider. Not 'It *won't* last' but 'It *might not* last'. Brad was willing to give their relationship as lovers a chance to deepen and grow, but he was warning her not to expect automatic permanence. That he cared enough to try was all she need to hear.

'My eyes were opened wide while you were in Calgary,' she said, running her hands over the corded muscles of his back. 'I want this, Bradley. No strings attached.'

He hesitated. 'This isn't a game I've won, Gwen.'

'No game. Just—intimate friendship.'

Still Brad hesitated, and Gwen wondered why. Did he realise that she would never take this step unless she had strong feelings for him? Had she somehow given away how she felt and now he didn't want to get involved, afraid that she'd cling to him when he was ready to end it?

He spoke so quietly that she almost missed his words. 'I have feelings, too, Gwen, and fears. Give me time to sort them out.'

Her heart contracted with unspoken love at this glimpse of his vulnerability. 'I will, Bradley. As much time as you need.'

He bent his head and his lips danced provocatively across her cheek. 'Do you think we can wait one more night?' he quizzed, dissolving the intensity of emotion between them.

'We could try,' Gwen said, moving her head to locate that elusive mouth.

She found it, and Brad's tongue immediately

thrust between her parted lips to partake of the honey inside. She tunnelled her fingers through his hair and pulled his head closer, revelling in the contact of his mouth and body on hers, inciting him, with the play of her tongue, loving him with her total being

'Do you call this trying?' he muttered.

'I call this kissing.'

'I call it torture.' Brad rolled on to his back, settling her snugly against his side. 'Gwen?'

She had nestled her head on his shoulder, and his breath was warm on her forehead. 'Hmm?' she said sleepily.

'I missed you, too. A lot.'

His admission banished any doubts Gwen might have had about the wisdom of her recent decision. Happy and content and ready to dream, she curled into his arms as if she'd been doing it for years and went to sleep.

Bright sunshine awakened her. Or was it the hand stealing a path up her thigh beneath the prim flannel of her nightgown? She slapped her palms against Brad's chest and arched away from him. Her reaction did not even remotely resemble the true nature of her feelings at waking up and finding the man she loved right there beside her.

'Don't do that, Bradley,' she warned. 'You know we don't have a lot of discipline when it comes to this.'

'I like this novelty of waking up with you beside me,' he said lazily. His hand was travelling higher. 'Kiss me good morning, Gwen.'

She resisted the pressure of his other hand on her back for a few seconds, then suddenly melted into him, her arms sliding around his neck as her mouth sought his. He eased on to his back, his strong arms lifting her body so that she lay on top of him. The nightgown was now up around her hips and Brad's hands were exploring her bare skin with erotic freedom. Hunger made her shift against him and his hands bit into her hips.

'You keep moving like that and we're not going to wait,' he threatened beneath his breath.

Gwen tore her mouth from his and the next instant was standing on the carpet beside the bed, her nightgown back down around her shaky legs. She drew in a deep, steadying breath.

'Bring me back some clothes, will you, sweet?' said Brad, flinging the covers to the foot of the bed and crossing to the bathroom.

Gwen turned resolutely away from the sight of his bronzed, hair-roughened legs and firmly muscled torso. This was going to be a very long day. They spent it avoiding each other, until early evening, when Brad came up behind her as she gazed unseeing at the open book in front of her. Why had he needed an extra day? She had told him she had made up her mind. Why couldn't he accept that? Why couldn't he make up his mind? He had been keen enough before. Brad's hand touched her shoulder and she jumped.

'I can't stand this any longer,' he whispered, and the strain was evident in his voice.

'Neither can I,' she replied, turning into his arms.

'Your bed or mine?' he murmured, his mouth playing absolute havoc with Gwen's senses.

'Which one's closer?' she asked breathlessly, no thought in her mind of pulling back. She wanted her husband. All of him. Tonight. Now.

The doorbell rang, and Brad swore. Gwen sighed.

'Who do you suppose that is?' she asked.

'I don't know and I don't care.' Brad's hands massaged her hips, drawing them forward against the male thrust of his. 'We have more important things on our minds.'

Gwen sought his descending mouth, hungry for the kisses she had by now come to regard as her right, just as it was her right to let her hands wander freely over her husband's body, searching for all the tempting areas that had been off limits to her before. She slipped a hand inside the back waistband of Brad's jeans, rubbing caressingly at the sensitive base of his backbone. He made a growling sound in his throat and transferred his mouth to her ear on a bridge of nipping little kisses.

The doorbell rang again.

'Bradley, we should see who it is.'

'No.'

Gwen arched away from his marauding mouth. 'It's probably the manager. Anyone else would have been announced by the security guard.'

'Then the manager can go bother someone else. We're busy.'

'Maybe it's important.'

Brad lifted his head, his blue eyes dark with shaded desire. 'Dammit, Gwen, we've stopped ourselves before and each time anger and misunderstanding have followed. Do you want to go through all that again?'

'He knows we're in here, Bradley.' A third ring sounded to confirm Gwen's statement. Reluctantly, she withdrew her hands from beneath Brad's sweater and smoothed it back down around his hips. 'It'll only take a minute to get rid of him. I can't—do what we're doing with a doorbell ringing continuously in the background.'

'One minute, then, no more. *Whoever* it is.' On that warning, Brad released Gwen so she could go and see who their visitor was.

It was Leo Bennett. Gwen stared at him in sheer surprise. 'Leo!' she exclaimed.

He gave her a big hug and handed over a bottle of champagne. 'Sorry to barge in on you like this, but I was in town and thought I'd come see your new home before heading for the airport to catch my plane.'

'Thank you, Leo, but you don't need to have an excuse to visit me.'

'Especially such a lame excuse as that one,' a laconic voice spoke up behind Gwen.

She turned to see Brad lounging in the foyer entrance-way, hands in his pockets, open mockery on his face. He straightened and strolled forward to stand beside her.

'I'm Brad,' he told Leo. 'Your god-daughter's husband. I hope you're not staying.'

'Bradley! He *is* my godfather.'

'I said *whoever* it was, Gwen, or have you conveniently forgotten?'

She stood indecisive, torn between the desire to finally make love with her husband and her duty towards their uninvited guest. Good manners won out. 'That—other matter—will just have to wait, Bradley,' she said, praying he'd understand and be patient just a little while longer. 'I'm sorry.'

'That's funny. You don't look at all sorry.'

'Bradley, you must know that I feel the same as you do,' she flared, annoyed that he thought her passion so shallow and easily replaced.

'Do you, Gwen?'

Leo looked from one to the other. 'Did I arrive in the middle of something?' he asked cautiously.

'A marital spat,' Brad answered. 'Don't let it bother you. We have them every day. Twice on Sundays,' he added with a satirical twist to his mouth.

'Pay no attention to him, Leo,' said Gwen, drawing her godfather inside. 'Come downstairs to the living-room. Would you like something to drink?'

'A cup of coffee would be nice. It's cold outside, feels like it might snow.'

Brad accompanied them downstairs and stayed to listen to their discussion of Leo's latest trip. Gwen mistrusted his silence, in particular the little smile on his lips. Brad caught one of her suspicious glances and immediately ran his gaze suggestively over her body. She shifted uncomfortably. Damn the man! He was seducing her with his eyes.

'And where are you flying to next, Leo?' she asked when the topic of Japan had been thrashed out and it was still too soon to courteously dismiss her godfather.

'Europe.'

'More business, no doubt,' Brad said politely.

'Always business,' Leo agreed.

'Were you responsible for your god-daughter's decision to study commerce?'

'Gwen has a mind of her own. I merely give her advice.'

'Oh, is that what you call it? And did you advise her on the merits of her marriage to me?'

'Leo only found out about it that night at the

restaurant,' Gwen spoke sharply. 'I told you that, Bradley.'

'So you did. I forgot.'

'You did not. You're just being difficult.'

His blue eyes gleamed at her. 'Shall we have another fight?'

'No, don't——' Leo began hastily. He was ignored.

'I'm ready to fight any time you are, Bradley,' Gwen said dangerously, rising to the bait.

'Fine. How about our renegotiating your allowance? Given your—shall we say so far limited—contribution to our marriage, what do you think you're actually worth?'

'A whole lot more than you could ever pay!' Gwen stood up quickly, struggling to hold back tears, too upset to question the surprising cruelty of Brad's remarks. 'I hate you, Bradley Robilliard! You're mean and arrogant and I wish I'd never married you!'

She ran upstairs to her room and flung herself face down across her bed, tears pouring down her cheeks and falling unchecked into her pillow. She cried for her dead parents, who she would never see again. For her brother-in-law, Bob—kind and gentle dreamer, but a weak man, too. For Naomi's suffering, borne with such determined good cheer and the never-failing belief that she would one day walk again. For little Julia, and her grandparents. And she cried, too, for herself. She was empty, so empty. She needed Brad to fill her life with his caring and teasing and constant presence, had thought she'd had him. Oh, God, why couldn't he need her, too? Love her? He would have so much, always, for the rest of his life.

'Gwen.' He was there, sitting down on the edge of the bed, rolling her over and lifting her across his lap. He cradled her in his arms, rocking her gently. 'I didn't mean it, Gwen, I didn't mean it. Please don't cry, sweetheart. I'm a bastard, and I say a lot of things to hide my real feelings. I didn't mean it.'

'I know.' Her arms encircled his waist and she buried her tear-drenched face in his shoulder. 'I know you didn't, Bradley. And I didn't mean what I said.'

'I know, honey.'

She clung to him, afraid that if she let go it would be the last time she would ever hold him. His hand stroked her back comfortingly as he waited for the last of her tears to subside. Finally, she drew in a shuddering breath and straightened away from his chest.

'What are we doing to each other, Bradley?' she asked in a broken half-whisper.

'A hell of a lot, and getting nowhere doing it.' He handed her a Kleenex from the box on the night table and she blew her nose. 'For every step forward, we take two or three back. We must be doing something wrong.'

'Where's Leo?' she asked, sniffing.

'I got rid of him, cutting short a splendid and quite detailed account of all my faults and shortcomings, both real and imagined.'

Gwen raised her head and met his eyes with a look that held no hesitation, no uncertainty. 'Then let's do something right, Bradley. Right now. Right here.'

He held her gaze for a moment, then slowly touched a gentle kiss to her lips. Not hesitant, but suddenly just a little shy, Gwen lowered her gaze to her fidgeting hands. Long brown fingers closed around them, lifted them to broad shoulders. Blindly, she raised her head to meet Brad's descending lips. Their touch was familiar, reassuring her. She sank pliantly backward as he pressed her to the pillows. Their hands undressed each other, their mouths teased. When cool air touched her naked flesh, Gwen breathed Brad's name longingly. He drew back a little and smoke-blue eyes roamed over her slim curves with the brand of possession, causing her to blush self-consciously. Her hands fluttered up instinctively to cover herself, but Brad caught them easily and bent his head to kiss each finger, then her palms, then the insides of her wrists.

'You're lovely,' he said, velvet lips against satin skin.

She shivered as the trail of fire moved down her arms and found the firm roundness of a breast. His mouth brushed across its rosy peak and continued on to the other one, this time pausing to taste and savour. Erotic delight shot through her, scattering her senses. Her hands gripped Brad's shoulders and she pushed him on to his back, leaning over him to rain hot, passionate kisses on his face. He lay still for a moment, turning his head so she could reach more elusive places. Then his hands came into play, gliding with slow, deliberate strength down her creamy shoulders, along the curve of her spine, over her smooth bottom to the sensitive skin of her thighs. Responding to his gentle pull, she settled her weight half on him, her knee hooked across his legs. His mouth caught hers in its heat, demanding and getting a total response.

Suddenly, without breaking contact with her lips, Brad flipped her neatly on to her back, reversing their positions. And with the change came active desire, thundering over them in a tidal wave and drowning them in its swirling current.

'Bradley,' she moaned, arching away for a moment from his rough, skilful hands and seductive mouth. 'Bradley, please, I've never done this before.'

His lips brushed her forehead. 'All right, sweetheart. Take it easy.'

And he was gentle with her, teasing her body into a natural response, arousing the melting need that would help her accept him, so that when they finally came together there was no tension, but only a deep, welcome sense of fulfilment. He gave her a moment to treasure it, smiling faintly down into her wide green eyes. Then he was moving, and it was being followed by a new building sensation that brought soft, wondering sounds from Gwen's throat. Her hands trailed down his shoulders and back to his hips, exploring, kneading, holding. There was no hurry. Brad let her revel in the experience, teaching her by example how to share it with him, murmuring soft encouragement in her ear.

Gradually, their union shifted to a more demanding level, leading Gwen into heavy territory. She rose to master it, hardly aware of the breathless words of passion being dragged out of her. And when the explosion of feeling came, her groan of exquisite pleasure was followed almost simultaneously by Brad's own, so that they reached the heights together, collapsing, a long eternity later, spent and breathing hard, in the mutual security of each other's arms . . .

Brad stirred, causing Gwen to murmur a protest. He pressed her head back down on to his shoulder. 'Lie still. I'm just turning out the lamp.'

Darkness flooded the room, wrapping them in a cocoon of intimacy. Gwen snuggled closer, sleepily curving her arm around Brad's waist as he pulled the blankets up around them. A kiss grazed her temple.

'Are you all right?' His voice was husky, content.

'Mmm. Bradley?'

'Yes?'

'Is it always like that?'

'Always like what?'

Gwen heard the smile in his voice. 'Never mind,' she said, a bit ruffled that he was teasing her.

He tightened the circle of his arms. 'With us, yes, it will always be like that. Even better.'

There was a relaxed silence between them until a thought chased away the languorous warmth stealing over Gwen. Her hand left Brad's waist and feathered a path up his hard, damp chest to the pulse beating at his throat. She whispered the thought aloud, with wistful regret.

'We'll have to get a divorce now, instead of an annulment.'

Brad's arms crushed her to him. 'Go to sleep, Gwen, and don't talk any more, okay?'

'Okay.'

She nestled against him. He had been her day and was now her night. Everything was as it should be. On a sigh of contentment, she turned her face into his throat and slept.

CHAPTER EIGHT

SNOW fell softly against the window panes, clinging to the glass and creating small patterns before sliding noiselessly down out of sight. Gwen stirred sleepily, started to stretch, and became abruptly aware of the masculine limbs entangled with hers. She turned her gaze to the left and saw Brad's tousled fair head on the pillow next to hers. A deep surge of happiness gripped her body and rippled through, leaving every nerve-end tingling. Feeling far too exuberant to remain still a second longer, she eased away from Brad's hold and slipped out of bed.

Brad changed position, rolling on to his stomach, one arm flopping out to lie across the space she had just occupied. He murmured something in his sleep, and the arm moved restlessly. Searching for her? Gwen waited to see if he would awaken, but he merely pulled her pillow under his arm and burrowed his face in its soft warmth. She gave him a smile full of love. He was so sweet. She leaned over and drew the covers up over his naked shoulders, pausing to drop a tiny kiss on the back of his head.

In the bathroom, she stopped to study her smiling reflection in the big mirror that stretched across the width of the wall above the vanity counter. Her gaze travelled slowly over her image, looking for changes. She touched hesitant hands to her breasts, then trailed her fingertips down over her stomach to her hips, her thighs. Her smile faded as doubts returned. Did she regret what she had let happen last night? Had she done the right thing? Tingling memories came back to her. She felt again Brad's exploring kisses, Brad's hands caressing her body, Brad filling her with delicious sensations that had left her limp with satisfied exhaustion afterwards. No, she didn't regret it. It had been everything she had hoped and longed for, and

more. She and Brad had, indeed, finally done
something right in their roller-coaster relationship, and
Gwen had a deep sense of conviction that they were at
last heading in their fated direction.

'Good morning,' came a soft greeting behind her.

Her eyes flew to the reflection Brad made over her
shoulder. He was leaning against the bathroom door-
jamb and for a brief instant emerald green met and held
brilliant blue. Then Gwen was whipping around to grab
a large bath sheet from the towel rack. She hurriedly
wrapped its concealing folds around her, not looking at
Brad, wretchedly aware of the hot blush suffusing her
cheeks. Being nude in his presence while he was asleep
was one thing; having him wide awake and watching
her was quite another.

'Gwen, don't. Sweetheart ...' Brad was in front of
her, his hands on her hips drawing her against him.
'Gwen, look at me.' Gentle fingers tipped her chin up.
'Last night wasn't a mistake, was it?'

'Bradley, no,' she said, startled that he was so attuned
to the workings of her mind. 'Of course not. It's
just ...' She cast a fleeting look up at him before fixing
her gaze on an invisible point somewhere behind him.
'It's—past eight o'clock, Bradley. You're going to be
late for work.'

A hand caressed her lower spine. 'Kiss me good
morning,' he said softly, moving his lips to the black
silk of her hair.

Gwen glanced sharply downward at her hands
clutching the two edges of the towel to her chest. Brad's
fingers were running lightly over the upper curve of her
breasts, sending responsive shivers through her body.
She pulled the towel up higher and heard his low
chuckle.

'I'm going to enjoy persuading you out of this
shyness of yours, Gwen,' he said. And then, 'Damn
Allegra for scheduling a nine o'clock conference for this
morning!'.

Strangely, Gwen felt no embarrassment at his own
nudity, perhaps because he was so unselfconscious
about it himself. 'I'll—go make breakfast while you

shower and dress,' she said, clamping down on the urge
to reach out for his body.

At the bathroom door a sudden impulse seized her.
Brad was taking a couple of towels from the wicker
shelf and with a little run she returned to reach up and
give him a quick kiss on the mouth. 'Good morning,
Bradley.' And then she was walking swiftly out of the
room, but not before she'd seen the beginning of a smile
on his face.

At the front door a short while after finishing his
breakfast, Brad bent his head to kiss her goodbye. 'Will
you be here when I get home?' he asked lightly.

They looked at each other, knowing the real question
on his mind. He was afraid their lovemaking had been
too great a step for her to take without a stronger
commitment from him.

'I'll be here, Bradley,' Gwen told him with quiet
reassurance. 'I promise.'

Relief flickered in his eyes. 'Good. Give me another
kiss.'

He took it—a rather long one—and then with a
hurried glance at his watch and a quick goodbye, he
was striding off down the corridor.

Gwen spent the day in a flurry of happiness, totally
caught up in optimistic dreams about the future. She
stayed home from classes and pored through the
cookbook Brad had unearthed from somewhere,
choosing several new dishes to serve during the special
dinner she was planning for that evening. The
apartment was attacked with spick and span energy,
and large bows were bought for the unsuspecting
kittens. The choice of what to wear took great thought
and prompted many changes of clothing to see what
would suit the mood best. By six o'clock she was
dressed, the table set, the meal almost ready, and the
kittens halfway to freedom from their hated bows.

Brad didn't come home.

Gwen anxiously checked all the clocks in the
apartment. They all read six twenty-eight. Maybe he
was just late.

An hour later the clocks read seven-thirty. Brad was

more than late. He was now in deep trouble, doubly so because he hadn't phoned to notify her or explain the reason. Gwen paced the length of the open area below the foyer, arms folded across her chest and a scowl on her face. To forget her birthday had been understandable, but to forget his own? Or was he out celebrating with someone else? Miss Company Treasurer, for instance? After all the trouble she'd gone to, the hot stove she'd *slaved* over, the fight she'd had with the kittens to get those dratted bows fastened around their necks, even the fact that she'd kept it secret that she even knew it was his birthday. The rat! He could turn thirty-three all by himself, then, if that was what he wanted.

By nine o'clock the cold food had been thrown out, the tableware put away, and the freed kittens enthusiastically destroying their bows.

By eleven-fifteen Gwen was in bed, silently simmering in the darkness.

At exactly three minutes past midnight, her door suddenly flew open and Brad staggered in. Gwen bounced up in shock, not having heard any sound of him entering the apartment. No light shone behind him, so he had obviously made his way to her room in the dark, and was now zeroing in on her bed with a like accuracy.

'Bradley——' she began ominously, and stopped when she made out the shape of a bottle in his hand. That he was quite drunk was evident in his stumbling walk and in his slurred words when he spoke.

'Bedtime. Past bedtime. Gotta sleep.'

He reached the other side of the bed, raised the bottle to empty what little contents remained, and then, dropping it to the carpet, collapsed heavily on to the mattress beside her. Gwen stared down at him in consternation.

'Bradley!' She prodded his shoulder. 'Bradley, get up!' But getting up was impossible for him, and would be for some time to come—he was apparently out cold. 'Oh, for heaven's sake,' Gwen said crossly. Then her face softened and she reached out to brush the hair from his forehead. 'My sweet, darling Bradley, what am I going to do with you?'

What she did was undress him, divesting him of shoes and socks, shirt and slacks—a difficult task when he was such a dead weight. Puffing slightly, she eased him back down against the pillows and then moved to the foot of the bed to pull the covers out from under him. But his body was clad only in black briefs now and she couldn't help pausing to study him in loving detail.

'You're absolutely gorgeous,' she said aloud, with no fear of his hearing her frank avowal. She drew the covers up over him, following with her body until the blankets were tucked beneath his chin and she was stretched out on top of him. 'I've got you now,' she said softly. His mouth caught her attention and she dropped a kiss on to it. 'Did you like that? Here's another one. And another.' She trailed a line of butterfly kisses along his jawline to his ear, enjoying this brief opportunity to touch him again, kiss him, without his knowing it.

But Brad reacted even while sunk in stupor, much to her alarm. His arm struggled free of the restricting blankets and with an indistinct mutter he rolled over with her until they were lying face to face on their sides. Impatient hands fumbled at the blankets separating their bodies. 'Witch,' he muttered. 'Damned, seductive witch. I want to feel you.'

Realising that he was more asleep than awake, Gwen forgave him his missing his birthday party and scrambled beneath the covers to join him. Immediately his hands were all over her, searching out every curve, pressing her to him. Long fingers hooked under the elasticised neckline of her nightgown and dragged it down one shoulder so his hand could close over her breast. A murmur of satisfaction left his lips and he settled more comfortably on the mattress, cradling her against him in one arm, his other hand in heavy possession of her breast. Gwen covered his hand with her own and snuggled closer.

'Happy birthday, Bradley,' she whispered, kissing his shoulder.

The next moment her contentment vanished and was

replaced with humiliation as Brad stirred briefly and mumbled a familiar name. Gwen shot upright and, in uncontrollable reaction, twisted around to deal his face a wrathful smack with her hand. So he thought he was in bed with Corinne, did he? Her fist came down hard on his unprotected stomach, causing him to give a low, protesting groan in his sleep.

'Damn you!' she said stormily.

She flung back the covers and jumped out of bed, furiously pulled her nightgown back up over her shoulder. So much for his 'Give me more time, Gwen.' While she'd been patient waiting for him to *sort out his feelings* as he'd asked, he had been indulging those feelings with his ex-girl-friend or current girl-friend or whatever she was. And Gwen's thought, never really given credence, that he had been celebrating his birthday with Corinne Mason had been all too correct after all.

Hurt and self-loathing jostled with fierce hatred for her husband in her mind. She felt like rolling him off the bed and stamping all over him, then told herself that he wasn't worth the effort. But that didn't mean he had to be comfortable in *her bed*! She leaned over to yank the pillow out from under his head, grabbed her own and dragged the quilt and bedspread away, leaving only the top sheet to cover him.

'And I hope you freeze to death!' she roundly told his sleeping form.

She marched to the den with her pile, slammed the door shut behind her as hard as she could, and curled up under the quilt and bedspread on the sofa. She was unable to go back to sleep, but spent the following wakeful hours profitably engaged in thinking up dire thoughts of vengeance against her stupid, uncaring, disgusting brute of a husband.

The next morning, Tuesday, Gwen awoke late with stiff muscles from her short bed. Her first thought was of Brad and his drunken behaviour. 'I hate him!' she said fiercely with convincing emphasis.

She got up and went back to her room, trailing the

blankets and two playful kittens. Brad was sprawled out on her bed, the top sheet tangled around his feet. Gwen threw him a black look and dropped the blankets to bang open the doors of her closet. Ignoring the low moan behind her, she pulled down a suitcase and began stuffing clothes into it, muttering to herself all the while.

'Come back to bed.'

She whirled at the huskily-spoken words to find Brad awake and watching her with sleepy attention. Indignation rose within her and she flung a sweater at him in a temper. It landed well short of its target.

'You're out of practice,' he grunted, struggling to sit up.

'And you're drunk—disgustingly drunk! You're also in my bed.'

'So come kick me out.'

Gwen angrily resumed her task, knowing that the moment she got within arm's length of Brad he'd have her right on that bed with him.

'Where do you think you're going?' he demanded.

'Out.'

'The hell you are. Put that suitcase away.'

Gwen cast him a scathing glance. 'I'd like to see you try and make me, the shape you're in!'

Brad swung his long legs to the floor and rubbed a hand wearily over his face. 'A slight hangover does not render me incapable of handling you, Gwen,' he said in a muffled voice.

'Handling me!' A rolled-up pair of slacks sailed through the air next. 'I am not an animal to be *handled*! And for your information I slept in the den last night, after you practically *pushed* me out of my own bed.'

He looked up, a frown drawing his brows together. 'The den?'

'Yes, the den. And the next time you get soused go to someone else's bed instead of mine!' Giving a haughty toss of her head, Gwen walked from the room with as much dignity as a long flannel nightgown and bulging suitcase would allow her.

*   *   *

Late the next afternoon Kelly James arrived in town, breezily saying that she had come to do some decent shopping in Vancouver's stores. Gwen had sought shelter with another friend, and from the speaking look Ingrid and Kelly exchanged, it was obvious that the latter's mission was two-fold. Sure enough, in short order she had Gwen spilling her troubles.

'Of all the nerve!' Ingrid exclaimed, when the story was finished. 'Having a mistress as well as a wife! Men are so selfish.'

Kelly was looking thoughtful. 'This is very interesting. Very interesting, indeed. The Brad you're talking about doesn't sound like the Brad I met.'

'I thought you said he was cold-hearted,' Gwen said resentfully. Kelly was supposed to be on *her* side!

'I did say that.'

'Then he's *just* like the Brad you met. He set out to seduce me, and the moment he succeeds, he tosses me over like old news.' That was an exaggeration, Gwen knew, but she wasn't in the mood to belabour the point. Brad had spent the night before last with her arch rival and he deserved all the slander she could think of.

'Liking kittens and afghans and your cooking argues a far from cold heart,' the redhead said decidedly.

'He was just pretending to like them, and what's wrong with my cooking?'

'If Brad hasn't told you, I will likewise refrain. But it doesn't surprise me that he took over.'

'And the kittens?' Gwen challenged, unwilling to allow Brad any saving graces.

'Try and take Bomber away from him and see how much he objects.' Kelly shook her head as one finding it hard to believe something she'd been told. 'Brad with a kitten—that I've got to see!'

'What about his behaviour with Gwen?' Ingrid spoke up, refilling their coffee cups. 'That has to mean something.'

'You're right, it does.' Kelly picked up a banana from the fruit basket in the middle of the table. 'It means he's absolutely besotted with her, that's what it means.'

Both girls stared at her.

'No,' whispered Gwen, hope dawning.

'Yes,' Kelly stated definitely, peeling her banana.

'I don't know,' Ingrid said with heavy doubt 'Isn't besotted too strong a word? Myself, I'd be inclined to think he's merely in love with her.'

Gwen looked from one to the other of her friends. 'But he was with Corinne that night——'

'Did he tell you that in so many words?' demanded Kelly.

'He said her name in his sleep,' Gwen answered stubbornly, which to her was as great a crime as his actually sleeping with the woman.

'For heaven's sake, sport! Didn't you even *ask* him where he'd been?'

'No, I didn't. He would have come up with some excuse that was supposed to satisfy me.'

'They all do,' Ingrid nodded wisely.

Kelly tossed the banana peel at her. 'You're not being a great big help, Ingrid.'

'That was a joke,' the other girl explained.

'Depressed people don't like jokes, and Gwen is depressed.' Kelly turned back to the matter at hand. 'Now, sport,' she advised with authority, 'Brad has a perfectly good reason for his whereabouts the night before last. Ask and you shall receive. As for his not loving you, I can see that he does even if you can't. My God, all you have to remember is Brad helping you paint the laundry room, Brad cleaning out the oven, Brad giving up smoking for you, Brad making love to you—although I don't see how you could forget that last one. Have you seen Gwen's husband, Ingrid? What a body! And looks?' Kelly gave a silent whistle.

'No, I haven't,' Ingrid answered regretfully, returning the coffee pot to the stove. 'Gwen, make up with Brad so I can come over for a visit, will you? On second thoughts, if you don't want him, give him to me. If he's such a good housekeeper and cook, besides being considerate, kind to animals and homeless strangers—wait, though. Is he good in bed? This is an important point to consider . . .'

'Ingrid!' Gwen exclaimed.

'He's good all right,' said Kelly with a low chuckle, noting Gwen's telltale blush. Taking a bite of her banana, she left off teasing and stood up. 'I'll call him.'

'No!' Gwen rounded the table to grip her friend's arm. 'You don't understand, K.J.——'

'Do you love him, sport?'

'Yes, but——'

'And he loves you, I swear it. If he doesn't, I'll make him. That's what friends are for.'

Gwen's hand fell to her side. Was Kelly right? Did Brad really love her? If so, she'd done him a great injustice by believing he'd spent the evening with Corinne. He was probably furious with her now for walking out on him for no apparent reason, and who could blame him? Guilt washed over Gwen in great waves—until she remembered that if Brad had come home at six like he was supposed to, they wouldn't have spent these last two nights apart. And come to think of it, since when had Brad ever been less than fifty per cent to blame for their fights?

Kelly brought the phone on its long cord into the kitchen and Gwen hovered at her elbow, determined that Brad wouldn't be given the impression that she was begging to make up with him. 'Don't tell him I *want* to see him. Just say——'

Kelly waved a shushing hand and spoke into the receiver. 'Hello, Brad? This is Kelly James, your wife's loyal friend and supporter.' She raised her eyebrows in surprise and covered the mouthpiece with her hand to hiss, 'He actually said something pleasant to me! This is *definitely* not the Brad I met.' She returned to the conversation. 'Yes, I'm here. Listen, Brad, I'm sort of acting as Gwen's representative in hers and your separation. She desires to know the current status of her contracted agreement with you ... Well, all right, let me put it another way. Do you want her back or don't you?'

'Kelly!' Gwen tried to wrest the phone from her and was fended off.

'He says he wants you,' the redhead told her in an

aside. 'Brad, as a concerned friend of Gwen's, may I ask what your intentions are?' A slow smile spread across her face as she listened. 'You know, you aren't half as bad as you paint yourself. Half an hour, then? . . . She'll be ready. Goodbye!'

'Did he sound anxious?' asked Gwen.

'Not at all.' Her friend looked her over critically. 'Jeans and a sweater will not do. Reconciliations call for something more romantic, especially when a candlelit dinner is involved.'

He hadn't sounded anxious. Gwen's spirits took a nosedive. He hadn't been worried at all, not even a minute's worth. 'I don't want to see him,' she refused stubbornly.

'Of course you do,' Ingrid encouraged, gently guiding her to the bedroom. 'Half an hour, isn't that what you said, Kelly?'

'That's what I said. Brad said fifteen minutes. He's an impatient man.'

'Fifteen minutes!' Gwen flew to her suitcase and began rummaging through it. 'I didn't bring anything to wear. Oh, Kelly——'

'Calm down, sport. *Love!*' Kelly said to Ingrid, rolling her eyes heavenwards.

Minutes later Gwen was dressed in royal blue linen slacks and a white lace blouse with a black velvet bow tied at the collar. She fastened a narrow black belt around her waist and stepped into her high-heeled black shoes.

'Do I look all right?' she asked anxiously, nervous hands patting at her loose curtain of hair.

'You'll pass,' Kelly responded drily.

The entrance phone buzzed and Gwen's gaze ripped apprehensively to the bedroom doorway. Would Brad be glad to have her back, or had he changed his mind about giving this new relationship of theirs a chance?

'He's on his way up,' announced Ingrid, coming back into the room. 'He has a deliciously sexy voice, Gwen. I could listen to him all day. Ready?'

'No,' said Gwen.

'Yes,' Kelly emphasised.

A knock was heard on the door.

'Heavens!' Ingrid exclaimed, startled. 'He must have run up the three flights of stairs.' She went to let Brad in.

'Kelly, what if he doesn't——' Gwen began.

'He does. Now if you don't go out there, your husband will come in here. So move.'

Brad was standing in the middle of the living-room making idle conversation with Ingrid when they emerged from the bedroom. Gwen stopped in the doorway, aching to run into his arms.

'Here, give me that,' he said, taking the suitcase from Kelly. 'It must weigh a ton with all the clothes I saw Gwen throw in it.'

'Bradley?' Gwen whispered tentatively.

He held out his free hand with a faint smile. 'Let's go home,' he said. She crossed the room to place her hand hesitantly in his. He closed his fingers firmly around hers and moved towards the door, speaking to her friends over his shoulder. 'Thanks for your help, girls. I owe you one.'

'Keep her this time, will you?' Kelly said caustically.

'I intend to.'

Gwen mulled over this promise all the way home as Brad concentrated on driving through the blinding rain which had replaced the previous day's snow. He was so uncommunicative. Why couldn't he just say 'I love you, Gwen, and I want us to stay married for ever'? Saying he intended to keep her didn't tell her a thing except that he was possessive. Not that she minded possessiveness, if the explanation behind it were reasonable. Such as he couldn't live without her, or had been dying of loneliness while she was gone, or even that he missed their spirited altercations. She sighed. Maybe she should just be grateful that he'd bothered fetching her at all. At least they were together again, and hope could once more spring eternal in her breast. Until their next misunderstanding.

As they took the elevator up from the underground garage, Gwen finally spoke. 'I hope you fed my kittens while I was gone.'

'One of your kittens is my kitten, and yes, I fed them, *and* got another scratch for my efforts. Kiss it better?'

Brad held out the palm of his hand to display a red welt across its width. Gwen took it in both of hers and touched a kiss to the scratch. How could she have left this precious man even for two days? He was as necessary to her life as breathing.

'Bradley, I'm sorry,' she whispered against his palm. 'I should have talked things out with you. Running away is the coward's way out.'

The fingers of his other hand rose in a familiar gesture, tucking a wing of hair behind her ear. 'We'll talk, Gwen. Later.'

Brad was standing close to her, very close, causing her to picture what his tall, rangy body looked like with no clothes on. Yesterday morning seemed so long ago, the night before even longer. Feeling suddenly daring, she flicked the tip of her tongue across his palm, ending the intimate caress with a speculative glance upwards.

'Too bad the elevator's reached our floor or I'd make you back that up with something stronger,' Brad glinted down at her. 'Now I'll have to wait until we're inside our apartment.' The elevator doors whisked open and he gave her a little push out. 'Walk fast, Gwen.'

'Why?' she asked innocently. 'I'm in no hurry.'

'Would you rather we do it out here in the corridor?'

'Bradley!'

He laughed and slipped an arm around her shoulders as they headed for their suite, the pleasure of anticipation keeping their strides normal. Once inside, Brad dropped the suitcase and swooped, catching her up in his arms. He carried her into her room and set her on her feet next to the bed. His arms were hard about her, drawing her against his body. Gwen lifted her mouth to meet his kiss, and as she did so the memory of another woman's name on Brad's lips as he lay holding her rose to haunt her. It was too distressing to be quietly set aside. Realising this, she pushed against Brad's chest, loosening his arms from around her. They needed to talk now, not later.

'Why were you so late coming home Monday night,

Bradley?' she asked, looking searchingly into his eyes. It was a simple question, one that should have been her first words to him the next morning.

He cupped her face between his hands, drinking in her cherished features. 'Corinne Mason,' he said, and placed a finger against her lips when she started to speak. 'I found out that she'd been an accomplice in the company embezzlement. The police and I set her up that evening and managed to get a very incriminating tape of her confession.' His forefinger traced Gwen's mouth, his eyes following the delicate path. 'Instead of coming home to a wife who would understand my anger and sense of betrayal, I used drink as a way of dealing with my feelings. I forgot that I have you to turn to, after all these years of having no one.'

'Oh, Bradley!' Gwen's arms went around his waist and she hugged him close in comfort. She knew he blamed himself for trusting his company treasurer so implicitly, and a painful part of her wondered if Corinne's personal betrayal was more upsetting to him than her illegal transaction. Dreading to know, yet aware that it would influence whatever happened next, she made a tentative probe of Brad's feelings for the other woman. 'Will she go to jail?' she asked.

'I damn well hope so. People like Corinne think they can get away with anything. This had better not be one of them.'

Gwen leaned back to stare up at Brad in dawning realisation. 'You don't like her, do you?'

'Good Lord, of course not,' he replied, looking startled. 'I thought you knew that.'

'No, Bradley,' she said with dry self-mockery, 'I didn't.'

He shrugged his broad shoulders, in that one gesture utterly confounding every bit of jealousy Gwen had thought rightfully provoked. 'I escorted her to a few business parties under duress. Other than that, she was good at her job, and that's all I cared about.'

'You said her name in your sleep that night.'

'Must have been having a nightmare.' Brad cocked a quizzical brow at her. 'Don't tell me that's why you ran out on me? Because you were jealous?'

'Why did you think?' Gwen asked crossly, not sure how much of her feelings she should reveal to him.

'I thought you were mad because your husband came home drunk.'

'My husband has to do a lot worse than that to make me leave!'

Brad smiled faintly. 'I'll make sure he never does. He needs his wife at home with him.'

'Does he, Bradley?' Gwen asked wistfully, covering the hand still cupping her face.

He met her gaze, and she saw words struggling for a way out. They flamed briefly before dying a silent death. When he did speak, the words were different from what she thought she had seen in those blue depths.

'I saw the birthday cake in the fridge,' he told her. 'How much trouble am I in for ruining your surprise the other night?'

Gwen kept her disappointment from showing, reminding herself that she'd promised to let Brad take things slowly, realising that she, too, did not quite trust enough to reveal the total extent of her feelings. 'Well,' she said with attempted lightness, 'if you kiss me ninety-nine times, I might—just *might*—forgive you.'

He unfastened the black velvet bow at her throat, his eyes burning into hers. 'Ninety-nine, huh? I think I could manage that.' His fingers started on the buttons of her blouse.

Gwen undid a middle button of his shirt and slipped her hand inside, sliding her palm upwards until it came into contact with his flat nipple. She plucked at it gently and smiled when Brad closed his eyes in reaction. 'You'd better hurry,' she said softly, withdrawing her hand in order to dispense with his tie. 'It's been two whole days since I had one, and I may just die of starvation.'

'Not a chance. I'd save you at the last minute.' Brad slipped the soft material of her blouse from her shoulders. 'I promise, Gwen,' he whispered, bending his head to kiss her exposed collarbone. 'I promise.'

Slowly, without further words, they removed each

other's clothing and found again the deep satisfaction of being together, making love, revealing with their bodies what both were so hesitant to reveal in speech. They were good for each other, each giving back what the other gave, as soft and aggressive in bed as they were out of it. Needing, wanting, their bodies melded in a joining wrought by all the feelings they shared, causing an explosive culmination of the flesh and the heart and the soul that left each trembling in aftershock, stripped of all uncertainty as to how they felt yet still too wary, too achingly fearful, to face love head-on and let it lead them where it might.

CHAPTER NINE

THE last weeks of November passed into December, speeding by Brad and Gwen unnoticed. The two of them were lovers now as well as friends, husband and wife as well as roommates. They couldn't do enough for each other. Gwen left special love notes for Brad to find in unexpected places, notes that teased, and hinted at deeper feelings, notes that made him smile at odd moments of the day. He brought flowers home for her every evening. They went to bed early and got up late, studying and paperwork and swimming all forgotten. So were uncles and godfathers and friends and strangers. These were laughing days, passionate days, and they were brought to an abrupt ending by the one person who had been trying to get Brad and Gwen together in the first place.

Gwen had tried to put aside her need to have Brad love her. She knew he was on his way, could feel the intensity of his caring when they had made love and he simply held her silently, possessively in his arms. But he was cautious, a man obviously hurt badly in the past and needing reassurance that those wounds wouldn't be ripped open again. So Gwen trod softly, at last starting to trust him with her love yet not pressuring him with any declaration until she felt he was ready to hear it. Instead, she showed him in so many little ways that he mattered to her, that she needed him and wanted him. Yet despite her steady patience and the knowledge that Brad's love would not come easily, she still found herself searching anxiously for a sign, any sign, which would tell her that he needed her, too.

His interest in her family background would have been one such sign, but he never asked about it. Neither did he reveal any part of his own. This bothered Gwen a little, undermining a tiny part of her blossoming hope for the future. She tried to tell herself that Brad would

ask—and talk—when he was ready. Families—hers, his,
and possibly some day their own—were a part of the
permanent world, and permanence was what he needed
time to think about. However, time did not last for
ever, and in their case it lasted barely three weeks. The
date of her monthly allowance rolled around, and
Gwen knew that her reason for marrying Brad was due
for discussion if a further misunderstanding was not to
arise. And the subject of *their* family was, if she was
reading the signs correctly, of suddenly even greater
necessity.

So, on an afternoon in early December, she gathered
up her hopes and dreams and courage and caught a bus
to the downtown office building that housed Brad's
company. The suite of offices belonging to Robilliard
Enterprises was on the eighteenth floor. Gwen had
never been there before and looked around with interest
as she approached the reception area. Dark oak walls,
cream carpeting and royal blue cushioned chairs gave
an impression of subdued elegance mixed with
undoubted success. Various offices branched off one
side of the wide corridor as well as off the main
reception area.

'Good morning. May I help you?' the receptionist
asked with a smile.

'Yes, thank you. I'm Gwen Ro——' She broke off in
consternation. Did Brad's staff know of his marriage?

The receptionist's jaw dropped. 'Gwen—Robilliard?'

'Yes.' Obviously they knew. 'Is Brad free? I'd like to
see him if possible.'

'Mrs Robilliard?'

A startlingly beautiful young woman with long pale
blonde hair stopped beside Gwen, a stack of files in one
arm. Quiet grey eyes assessed her quickly, intelligently.
The woman smiled and held out her hand.

'I'm Allegra Wheeler, your husband's executive
assistant. He's talked about you often. It's a pleasure to
meet you at last.'

'Thank you,' said Gwen, shaking hands. She felt as
though the woman, who couldn't be more than three or
four years older than herself, had passed swift judgment

on her, and been satisfied with what she had found. 'Is
Brad in? He's not expecting me, but——'

'He's just finishing with a client. Why don't you come
and sit down? He won't be long.'

As Gwen walked towards the blue reception chairs
with the other woman she became aware of being the
focus of attention.

'You know him well?' asked Gwen, to take her mind
off what she was sure was a critical inspection from
Brad's employees.

'Well enough to know that he's in love with his wife,'
Allegra answered. The smile rose to lustrous grey eyes.
'I'm the one who has to rearrange all his appointments
whenever he arrives late for work in the morning!'

Soft colour tinged Gwen's cheeks. Their love making
had often made them both late—Gwen for classes, Brad
for the office. Allegra touched her arm.

'Don't mind me. I tease Brad, too.'

'Gwen?'

It was Trace Robilliard—tall, dark, forbidding.
Allegra's self-assurance seemed all at once to leave her.
She stood up hurriedly, clutching the files tightly to her
chest.

'I'll go buzz Brad and let him know you're here,' she
told Gwen, and walked rapidly away.

Trace stopped before her chair, his attention on
Gwen. 'I was talking to Brad on the phone yesterday.
He sounded strange, so I flew here this morning to see
him.'

She was puzzled. 'Strange? How do you mean?'

'He was happy. In our family, that's strange. I gather
you're responsible for it.'

Hearing two people remark, in the space of a few
minutes, on how happy Brad was increased Gwen's
faith in his eventual love for her by a gigantic leap.
Allegra, however, had been a lot more approving than
Trace seemed to be.

'We're both—very happy,' she answered, not sure of
her brother-in-law's attitude. He wasn't smiling.

'I consider myself an accurate judge of character,
Gwen, and the honesty of yours shines through pretty

brightly.' Trace stepped closer, towering over her. When he spoke again, his words were a soft threat. 'But if I'm wrong, and you hurt Brad, I'm going to break every bone in your body. My brother has already been put through the wringer by one woman. She got off scot-free, taking with her a hefty reward from our grandfather. You won't. Do you understand?'

Gwen rose to her feet. Strangely, this cold, dangerous man did not frighten her. She sensed in him what was in Brad—an absence of love, but also the potential to love with great depth once the barriers of distrust and remoteness were knocked down. She said quietly, 'Trace, I know Brad has been hurt badly in the past— it's all there in his eyes. Sometimes I catch him looking at me as if he's wondering whether I'll hurt him, too. But I won't. I can't. Hurting him would be like hurting myself, and both of us would suffer the pain. I love him, Trace—I can't begin to tell you how much. And I think he's falling in love with me. With his help, our marriage is going to *work*.'

He looked at her in silence for a long moment, then suddenly bent to brush her cheek with his lips. 'A belated kiss for the bride. And won't *that* make Brad's staff all agog—the brother hustling the wife!' He straightened, and Gwen could have sworn she saw a glimmer of a smile in those glacial blue eyes. 'Tell Brad that big brother is reassured and has gone off to mind his own business again.'

Trace swept an ironic glance around at the hastily averted stares of the employees before turning to leave. Gwen sat down again, but had only a minute in which to think back on her brief exchange with him before being hailed a second time. She raised her head, startled. The last place she had expected to see her godfather was in her husband's office.

'Gwen, what are you going here?' he asked, stopping in front of her.

'I've come to talk to Brad. More to the point, what are *you* doing here?'

'I suppose you and he have had another fight,' Leo sighed, and continued before Gwen could deny it. 'It's just as well that I ran into you. I would rather speak to you first, anyway. Come on, let's go some place where we can talk in private.'

He chose a small, empty office around the corner from the elevators, on the other side of the building, seeming to know his way around without difficulty. Gwen felt a slight twinge of apprehension.

'Leo, what's this all about?' she asked, once the door was closed behind them.

He walked to the window and stood with hands in pockets, his back to her. He was a careworn man with some heavy thoughts on his mind. 'Gwen, since that Sunday when I was at your and Brad's apartment, I haven't stopped thinking about your marriage.'

'Leo, that evening I was just——'

'You don't have to explain, Gwen. I saw the way Brad was with you, and I'm sure that was just a sample of how he's been treating you.'

'Believe me, Leo, I give as good as I get——'

He held up a hand, his attention still on the view outside. 'Please, let me finish. I've been guilty of trying to manage the lives of two people I care very much about, and have only succeeded in making them both unhappy.' He turned to face her. 'This may come as something of a surprise to you, Gwen, but Brad is my nephew.'

His nephew. Uncle. Leo was Brad's uncle. For a moment Gwen didn't quite grasp the significance of his disclosure, then it struck her. A surprise? She felt an almost hysterical desire to laugh. A high-voltage shock was more like it. She stared unseeingly at the opposite wall, trying not to let her mind explode with ugly suspicion, silently willing her godfather to stop talking. It couldn't be true. She would not listen, would not accept what it could mean. *Oh, Leo, don't do this to me. Please don't!*

But self-reproach had taken strong hold of Leo and he was determined to confess everything. He began pacing back and forth with a deep frown on his face, striving to explain, unaware of the lethal blow he was inflicting upon Gwen.

'I wanted you and Brad to marry because I was convinced the two of you were meant for each other, and the financial situation you were both in was a means to hasten the process. Don't tell me I shouldn't have done it, because I know that now, but when I looked at Brad, and then looked at you—it just seemed such a pity that you two weren't together. So I arranged for you to marry, never dreaming what a disaster it would turn out to be.'

More than a disaster. A destruction of everything Gwen had experienced with Brad. It had all been an act on his side. She knew it just as surely as if he were standing there and telling her himself. She felt her heart tearing at her chest, in mortal agony with no hope of being put out of its misery. In Leo's words were all the answers to Brad's behaviour, all the explanations. Why hadn't she been more suspicious, less willing to be satisfied with Brad's delaying tactics? Because she loved him, that was why, and had wanted him now, not when it suited him, if it ever did. And she was paying the price for it now. A savage, bitter price.

Leo stopped pacing and came to place his hands on her shoulders, sad regret in his eyes. There was nothing in her expression to indicate the effect his words were having on her. Her mind and face were blank, her feelings suspended. The world was spinning around her.

'I never meant for you to be unhappy, Gwen,' her godfather said sincerely. 'I thought you'd like Brad, and he you. Even after our dinner in the restaurant, I was certain you were both starting to care for one another. But when I found out you two were always fighting, when every time I talked to you on the phone you sounded so upset, I began to realise that for the first time in a long time I had misjudged a situation. It took that Sunday evening, though, to really open my eyes. Now I know what a huge mistake I made, and I'm ready to correct it.'

I don't want you to correct it. Oh, God, Leo, you're taking Brad away from me!

He hitched a hip up on the edge of the desk,

oblivious to Gwen's unspoken plea, blind to the fact
that the light in her eyes had been snuffed out. Leo was
wrecking her life, and he didn't even know it.

'You know,' he said, frowning, 'I told Brad at the
start that if he wasn't nice to you our loan agreement
would end. I guess he didn't take me seriously.'

Gwen flinched. Brad had taken his uncle seriously, all
right. Looking back, she could pinpoint the exact day
he had begun. Almost the exact minute.

*It's my turn to cook supper tomorrow. Do you like
stew?*

'And dumplings?'

*'Well, I'll try, just for you, but don't set your heart on
them.'*

Yes, that had been the start of Brad's 'niceness', and
everything that had followed was meant only to ensure
that she would stay the year required of her.

Gwen said through stiff, frozen lips, acknowledging
the truth as she spoke, 'His—company—means a great
deal . . . to him.'

'A very great deal,' Leo agreed. 'He could have gone
to his grandfather for the money, of course, but
Philippe did something to him years ago—what, I don't
know—for which Brad has never forgiven him, so he
must have figured you were the lesser of two evils.'

Was that really what she was to him? A lesser evil?
Gwen bowed her head, letting her hair fall forward to
hide her face. She was not going to cry, not yet, because
when she started she wouldn't be able to stop.

'Are you all right?' her godfather asked, suddenly
cognizant of her reaction to his news.

'Quite . . . all right.' She raised her head. Where the
smile came from she didn't know, but she gave him one.
'I'm still a little dazed, that's all. I hadn't realised how
easily you could end all my . . . troubles.'

'I would have done it sooner, but I kept hoping—
however, that's neither here nor there.' He sighed
heavily. 'I'll talk to Brad, tell him he can have my loan
without staying married to you. I'm sure he'll be
relieved to be let off the hook.'

'Yes. Yes, I'm sure he will be, too.'

'As for you, young lady, I'm not going to listen to another word about charity. I'm your godfather, and if I want to pay off those hospital debts, I will.'

'Thank you, Leo. I'm—very grateful.'

His voice became concerned. 'Is something wrong, Gwen? You look ill.'

'I—I woke up with a touch of the 'flu this morning. Or something.' What a word to call the fragile life stirring inside her! Gwen slid a protective hand to her stomach. 'Leo, do you think—could you take me home? I really am not feeling at all well.'

'Certainly I'll take you home.'

He was all solicitousness as he escorted her downstairs to a taxi, and thoughtfully silent during the ten-minute drive to the apartment. Gwen was thankful. She wouldn't have been able to hear a word over the blood rushing loudly through her veins, over the thunderous beat of her pulse and the sounds of her heart as it struggled not to break . . .

'Allegra, where's my wife?'

The blonde woman looked up from her desk in surprise. 'She was waiting in reception, Brad.'

'She's not there now,' he snapped. He'd been tied up with that damned slow-talking client longer than he'd expected. If Gwen had come to see him, why couldn't she have stayed until he was free? He raked his fingers through his hair. The entire day had gone badly. Seeing her would have made everything a lot better.

'Perhaps she's in the washroom,' Allegra suggested. 'I'll go check.'

Brad went back to his office. He had a premonition— crazy, when he'd never had one before. He sat down at his desk, attempting to shake it off.

Allegra returned to report no sign of Gwen. Everyone else had gone off for lunch, so there was no one to say where she might have disappeared to.

'Thanks, Allegra,' Brad said curtly. 'You go for your lunch, too.'

He picked up a report and tried to concentrate on the

information it contained. He was still trying when a knock came on his door and Leo Bennett walked in. The premonition grew stronger.

'This is a surprise, Leo,' said Brad, rising slowly to his feet.

'I'm here to talk to you about your marriage to Gwen,' Leo said abruptly.

'My marriage is private business between my wife and me.'

'Not when I'm responsible for letting you make her miserable,' his uncle said sternly, seating himself.

Brad frowned down at him. 'Gwen is not miserable.'

'You'd like to have me believe that, wouldn't you? Well, it won't wash. I saw her in reception earlier and we had a little talk. I told her I was your uncle and——'

'Why the *hell* did you do that?' Brad almost hissed the words.

'Because your marriage is over. I saw how upset Gwen was when I dropped by your apartment that Sunday. Knowing you, you've probably been insulting and browbeating her from the beginning. No wonder she said she hates you!'

Brad felt as if he'd been poleaxed. 'She said that?' The idea was so ludicrous that he didn't hear Leo's response, his mind reeling under the impact. He sank back slowly, every muscle tense, divided between a rising urge to murder either his uncle or his wife, depending on who would turn out worse. If she'd betrayed him, if she'd *pretended* . . . 'What exactly did Gwen say when you revealed your relationship to me, Leo?' he asked with a clinical detachment that cost him every scrap of self-control he had.

'I don't remember exactly what she said,' answered the ever-helpful uncle. 'I did most of the talking. She was surprised, of course. I expected her to be angry with me, but she didn't even——'

'What else did she *say*, Leo?'

'She said that all her troubles were ended. She agreed to my giving her the money she needed, and was clearly relieved that she could get out of the marriage so easily.

I wish I'd never arranged it in the first place. It's given me a whole new ulcer.'

It had happened again. Give a woman money and she ran out on you without a backward glance. *You damned fool. You damned, trusting fool.*

'In a way, I'm glad the marriage didn't develop as I'd planned,' Leo said conversationally, settling more comfortably in his chair. 'Gwen's always said she couldn't let anything interfere with her progress towards a high-level executive job. Personally, I thought she was too young to be so dead set on such a resolve, but I guess she's not going to change. Like you, it's business before pleasure with her. I don't think even love would take priority.'

'Then it's lucky I didn't fall in love with her,' Brad commented.

'I suppose so, now that I think of it. But then you're not the kind to fall in love, anyway, are you?' Leo asked quizzically.

Brad's gaze flickered away and then back. 'Far from it. Love holds no interest for me.'

'Thank God for that. I never would have forgiven myself if you'd fallen for Gwen when she so obviously loathes being married.'

He hadn't noticed any loathing. But then, a skilful little actress like she was would have been careful to hide her real feelings. 'Leo,' hc said casually, his eyes on his hands resting splayed and unmoving on the desktop, 'why did Gwen marry me?'

'You know why. She needed the money, and being the kind of girl she is, she would have done anything to get it—except take it from me.'

Brad felt a savage impulse to smash a dozen windows. 'Anything?'

'Absolutely,' his uncle affirmed. 'She'd go to hell and back if that's what it took. She's tougher than she looks, is my god-daughter.'

'So she once said.'

'Now, about the annulment——'

'Let me worry about that.' Brad rose. 'I have a meeting in five minutes, Leo, so if you'll excuse me . . .'

'Certainly.' Leo stood up. He had fixed everything right and tight and was in a cheerful mood. 'I'll be in town all day. Why don't the three of us—you, Gwen and I—have dinner together this evening to celebrate the parting of ways? If,' he added humorously, 'you two can put off fighting for a couple of hours.'

'Not tonight, Leo. I have a date. So does Gwen. Some other time, perhaps.'

Brad edged his uncle towards the door, deaf to the older man's departing conversation, his own words of farewell automatic and far away. He locked the door after Leo, walked to the drop-bar in the corner, took out a bottle of Scotch and a glass, sat down at his desk, and poured the first drink. And then just sat there staring at it. Drink wasn't the answer—not any more. Gwen was. But she wasn't there to turn to this time. She never really had been, more fool he. He leaned back in his chair and wondered how long it would take for the pain to stop. And he knew that it would be a very long time, and that it might just kill him first.

A rough little tongue licked at the tears on Gwen's cheeks. She opened her eyes and gathered Max in close. Bomber was balancing on the back of the sofa, uncertain. He was Brad's kitten. For an instant she felt that he had betrayed her, too, then she pulled him to her chest and buried her face in his soft fur. She'd been sitting in the cold living-room for hours, and only now were her tormented mind and heart beginning to accept the soothing calm of reasoned thinking. She had cried long and hard, had raged inwardly at a man filled with treachery, had fought a love that wouldn't die like she wanted it to. Now, exhausted and despairing, she straightened out of her miserable huddle on the sofa and allowed her thoughts to seek the truth.

The truth was bright and dark. Gwen loved her husband, and she wouldn't if he were as deceitful and callous as Leo's story had first made her believe. Yes, Brad had lied about not knowing her godfather, but his reason had to be just as good as her own in not revealing why she had needed the hundred and fifty thousand dollars. Distrust. Wariness. They'd been two strangers tossed together into close contact and had instinctively thrown up walls to protect the privacy of their thoughts and feelings, robbing each other of the opportunity to be honest and natural. The events that followed—the laughter, the fights, the caring—had taken place on shaky ground, and were tinged with whispers of doubt and suspicion that had kept them from building the solid foundation they needed in order to flourish.

Gwen rubbed her forehead wearily, the tears on her cheeks now dry and forgotten. Considering the fragility of their relationship, maybe she didn't know Brad as well as she thought. He was entirely capable of ruthlessness, and in his determined bid to save his company could easily have capitalised on her surrender to him, using it as a means to guarantee the security of his uncle's loan. And having fun while doing it, too, always intending to slip away from the clinging trap of her embrace the minute their one-year contract ended. Was that how he was? Warm and caring on the outside, but calculating and singleminded beneath the surface?

In the face of Leo Bennett's confession, Gwen was no longer certain of anything. Forced to marry by his uncle, possibly even guessing that the older man was matchmaking, Brad would have been ripe for a heartless cat-and-mouse game. Except that he had come to like the mouse. Gwen didn't doubt that. His teasing had been spontaneous, his tempers real, his concern genuine. For him, being nice to her turned out not to be the onerous task he'd no doubt envisaged. But where had it gone from there? If Brad was innocent of all ulterior motives, had he simply decided against becoming seriously involved with her and opted instead for the freedom of bachelorhood? He had certainly seemed satisfied to enjoy her friendship and company in bed with no apparent interest in anything beyond that point. Things like love, and anniversaries. And babies. Gwen pressed the back of her hand against her mouth to stifle a small, involuntary moan of despair. Brad had never talked about anything in the future—not her graduation from university next spring, not the question of her allowance, not even about Christmas now three weeks away—so what chance did anniversaries and babies have? Specifically, one little baby who might just be born around the date of their first, and possibly last, wedding anniversary?

She hugged the kittens tighter, tears welling up in her eyes again. She loved Brad and her love was not so shallow to believe the worst of him when all she had seen was the best. It was a deep love, irreversible and infinite, and it would trust in the man who had made it blossom and grow. Whatever his intentions might have been at the outset, Brad cared about her now, and he would not willingly give up the happiness he and Gwen were sharing. She just hoped that he realised it before the main consequence of their 'happiness' was revealed.

When Brad came home that evening, Gwen met him at the door with total faith in his sincerity and a readiness to untangle any knots that Leo might have wrought. It never occurred to her that her hamhanded godfather would not only have tangled the whole rope, but cut it cleanly in half when he was through.

'Bradley, I'm sorry I left your office before seeing you, but——'

He avoided the kiss she had stretched to give him and brushed past her, stopping at the bottom of the foyer steps to riffle through his mail lying on the hall table. 'I understand that your godfather—my uncle—has decided to forgo his subtle arrangement for giving you the money you want and simply hand it over directly.'

His chilly voice caused Gwen to stare at his back in consternation. 'Yes. Bradley, I——'

He interrupted her. 'Don't call me that. And let's forget the "It was fun while it lasted but now I have to go" stuff.' He tossed down his mail and turned to face her. 'I hate long-drawn-out goodbyes, don't you?'

She gazed at him numbly. This cold and isolated man was not her husband. 'Goodbye?' she whispered, refusing to believe what he seemed to be saying.

'Come now, Gwen,' he chided. 'You can't mean to continue living here with me? Thanks to Leo's last intervention, we no longer have any use for each other, and I'm sure you can find another apartment that suits you just as well. Just be sure to take all your afghans and plants with you, hmm?'

Stricken by what she was hearing, Gwen reached out a pleading, trembling hand to him. 'Bradley, what are you saying?' she asked in a tortured voice.

He knocked her hand away from his arm. 'Cut the little-girl-lost routine, Gwen. It won't work. Do you honestly think you can have Leo's money and mine, too? That really is ambitious of you! But I'm not so gullible. Our contract ended at twelve-fifteen this afternoon. I'm heading out on another business trip tomorrow, so you can stay here until the end of the month, but as of the thirty-first I'll expect you to be gone. Understand?'

His words ripped through Gwen, stunning her with their power to hurt. She looked at Brad and saw what she had seen on first meeting him—the cold eyes, the aloof features, the attitude that said 'I always go for what I want and to hell with anyone who gets in my way.' And, finally, her heart believed what her mind had been determined to tell it. Not that Brad had tricked her and used her—she still wasn't convinced of that—but simply that he didn't love her. And that knowledge cut deeper than any game of his ever could have. Head down, defeated and subdued, Gwen did not bother trying to fight back. Brad had buried the part of himself that she treasured, but the memory of it confronted her now, and she could not hurt something so precious and priceless. Neither could she leave him with the truth still unspoken and hidden. Unconsciously, she spoke an epitaph for the hopelessness of her love.

'Bradley, I've tried to understand you, and obviously failed,' she said in a low, constricted voice. 'You asked for time, and I gave it to you. It seemed it wasn't enough. I gave you my body, my heart and soul, and still you appear to want more. But you've drained me. I have nothing left to give. You've got it all.' She looked up, her eyes bright with unshed tears. 'I love you, Bradley. Maybe I should have told you that weeks ago.

Maybe that's what you needed to hear to start loving me back. But I didn't want to rush you, didn't want to scare you off. And now it's too late, isn't it? Somehow I've lost you. You've become a stranger again, someone I don't know. And——' Her voice broke at the memory of his cruel words, and a tear tumbled down her cheek. 'And, right now, you're someone I don't want to love.'

Green eyes drenched with grief, she stepped down from the foyer and walked away from Brad, her slender shoulders hunched with the burden of her loss.

'Gwen, don't go——'

She stopped at the slightly ragged sound of Brad's voice. She knew that despite his harsh words, he was suffering his own loss, but she didn't turn around to see it. To turn would be to give in, and perhaps trap him in a cage he couldn't bear. Time had run out. Now, Brad must make the first step—towards her, or nothing.

'I can't take any more, Bradley,' she whispered in soft anguish, staring down through her tears at her clasped hands. 'I'm going to my family in Toronto. If you want me, I'll be there. If not—be good to the kittens, will you?'

On a choked sob, she ran to her room and closed the door on what she had left behind.

CHAPTER TEN

THREE pairs of intent green eyes were fixed on five pink toes. Silence hung over the room. All breathing was momentarily suspended. The toes moved—slowly, with great difficulty.

'You did it, Mummy, you did it!'

'Oh, Naomi, that's wonderful!' Gwen rose on her knees to give her sister a fiercely loving embrace. 'It's incredible, it really is.'

'The doctors call me a miracle. Most of them swore I'd never be able to use my legs again.' Naomi patted the arm of her wheelchair. 'I will walk again, Gwen. I *will*.'

'I already *can* walk,' Julia bragged. 'See, Annigun?'

'Yes, honey, I see.' Gwen smiled affectionately at her stumbling antics. The braces were gone now, and Julia was like a newborn colt trying out legs that were as yet too shaky and clumsy for her needs.

'Julia, sweetheart, why don't you go out to the kitchen and see what Nana and Gramps are making for supper?' Naomi suggested. She gave her daughter a tiny smack on the bottom and watched smilingly as she limped heavily out of the bedroom. 'She's come a long way.'

'Like her mother. You're both tough.'

'It runs in the family.' Naomi reached out to smooth the collar of Gwen's blouse. 'Playing hide-and-seek with Julia has left you a little dishevelled.' She paused. 'How are you feeling?'

Gwen drew her legs up to rest her chin on her knees. 'I only have morning sickness about once a day now. I'm improving.'

'It's been three days since your suspicion was confirmed, Gwen. You should tell Brad about the baby.'

'No. He doesn't love me, doesn't care about me, so why should he care about the child we made?'

'He's going to know sooner or later. You're seven weeks pregnant. In a few months when you begin to show——'

'In a few months, when I begin to show, he won't be around to see it.'

Gwen rose to go to the window. Snowflakes fluttered against the glass. Beyond, everything was dark, except for the little tree strung with Christmas lights in the backyard. Christmas was over, New Year had passed. Soon she would be in Vancouver again, preparing to start her final term at university. Where was all the happiness, the enthusiasm and motivation? Her mouth trembled. Locked up, along with all the other good feelings. And she wasn't the one who had the key.

'You're going to leave Brad for good, Gwen?' Naomi asked worriedly.

'Yes.' She shoved her hands into the front pockets of her blue jeans and turned to lean back against the windowsill, her brooding gaze on her slippered feet. 'He married me for money and it seems as far as he's concerned, that's all our marriage was based on. A little sex thrown in was an added bonus for him. A lot of sex,' Gwen corrected herself on a mutter of recollection. 'I've agreed to accept Leo's help with the hospital debts, Naomi. There's such a thing as too much pride, and he really does want to help. We can pay him back over a period of time and——'

'*I'll* pay him back.'

'No,' Gwen said again, but this time she looked up with a faint smile. 'Said the little sister to the big sister. You might be out of that wheelchair by next summer, Naomi, but you'll still have a long way to go, and you know it. After I graduate, I'll get a job here in Toronto and start paying Leo back. The five of us can live in this house and manage just fine on my salary.'

'Aren't you forgetting something?'

Gwen's smile faded. No, she wasn't forgetting. The baby was due in early September. When she graduated she'd be six months pregnant and her chances of landing the type of job she wanted would be practically non-existent.

'You still love him, don't you?' The slow tears that gathered were all the answer Naomi needed. 'Oh, honey, I wish there was something I could do . . .'

'I'm all right. I just—I don't want to love him, Naomi, but I can't stop. I keep remembering all the little things we did together and—they make it hard to understand what went wrong.'

Neither spoke for a moment. Then the phone rang out in the kitchen, and Gwen pushed herself reluctantly away from the windowsill to go and answer it. Naomi motioned her back.

'Grandma or Grandpa will get it.'

The phone's third ring was cut off in the middle as someone lifted the receiver.

'Gwen, are you so convinced that Brad doesn't love you?' Naomi asked, troubled. 'From what you've told me——'

'He likes me, Naomi, more than a little. But love is so different, such a giant step from the safety of mere liking. Brad isn't willing to take that step. He proved that when he left the apartment that last evening and didn't come back. It killed any hope I might have had left.'

'But if he told you he was going on a business trip . . .'

'That's what he said.' Gwen hugged her middle as a chill seemed to grip her body, feeling again the huge gap in her life where Brad used to be. She hadn't succeeded in banishing him from her thoughts even a little bit. He was always there, in her memories, in her dreams. Would it never stop? 'I talked to his friend Shane a few days later before coming here,' she continued, steadying her voice. 'He'd just seen Brad at the office that morning, and didn't know anything about a business trip. So obviously that had been just another lie, like all the rest.'

'Or the result of one more misunderstanding,' Naomi suggested.

'No, not this time. I told Brad how I felt, and he should know me well enough by now to realise that I was being honest. That leaves me with only one conclusion: he doesn't share my feelings, and going back to him now, pregnant, would only trap him with guilt and responsibility. I can't do that to him, Naomi. And I won't do it to myself.' Gwen forced brightness into her face and voice as she crossed to her sister's wheelchair. Talking about Brad was not helping her inward battle to forget about him. 'Listen, I promised Grandma homemade biscuits for supper tonight. Why don't we enlist Julia's help and go make them?'

'You're on,' Naomi said promptly, knowing when a subject was meant to be dropped.

Gwen guided the wheelchair down the hall to the kitchen, Their grandparents weren't there, but Julia was, balancing on a step-stool and involved in her favourite pastime—talking on the telephone. Her back was turned to her mother and aunt, and her chattering hit them before either could say a word.

'She can't come to the phone right now cuz she's crying. Annigun is *always* crying. She has a baby, but I haven't seen it. Have you, Uncle Bwad?'

'Oh, my God,' Gwen whispered. 'Brad!' She ran to the phone and grabbed it out of her niece's hands, an arm automatically going around the little girl's waist to keep her secure on the step-stool. She whipped the receiver to her ear just in time to hear the click at the other end as the connection was abruptly broken. 'Brad? Brad——!'

'I told that man about your baby, Annigun,' Julia said importantly. 'He said he was your husband an' his name is Bwad, so he's my Uncle Bwad, isn't he?'

Gwen slowly returned the receiver to its cradle. The hammer had fallen. If Brad had called at all, it was to make that first step she'd wanted him to take. Now, he'd never complete it. A wife was one thing, a family—too much, too soon, He was out of her life now. For good.

Julia tugged at her sweater. 'Isn't he, Annigun?'

'What? Oh. Yes, sweetheart, he's your Uncle Brad.' *Or was, until a minute ago.* Gwen lifted her niece in her arms and sat down with her on her lap on the top step of the stool. She looked over the little girl's mop of black curls at Naomi, her eyes a deep, haunted green.

'It'll be a shock, Gwen,' her sister said softly. 'Give him time to get over it.'

'That doesn't work, Naomi. Brad is scared—of love, of me, and now of a baby, the strongest commitment to the future of them all. If he comes to me now, it'll only be to discuss arrangements for the support of his child.' And Gwen closed her eyes against the pain that was cutting her to the soul.

'What are you going to do?' asked Emily Shaughnessy, placing a pile of carefully folded clothing in her granddaughter's suitcase.

Gwen picked up a stray shoe. 'Leo's found me a furnished apartment close to the campus. I'll pack up my things while Brad's at work and move into it, then start my last term at university.'

'Are you going to try and see Brad?'

'No, Grandma. I told you, our marriage is over and done with. So let's—not talk about it any more, please?'

'All right, dear. It's just that I hate to see you so unhappy.'

'I know, Grandma.'

Gwen glanced around the guest room to see if she'd forgotten to pack anything. Brad's aborted phone call last night had signalled the end of their relationship, and her decision to return to Vancouver had soon followed. Leo, while not knowing any more than he already did, understood her desire to leave Brad's home, and had swiftly and efficiently gone about finding his cherished godd-aughter a place to live. His generosity extended to Gwen's living expenses for the rest of her university term and more than enough money to pay off the remainder of the hospital debts and any other bills Naomi's recovery would incur.

Gwen smoothed a restless hand over her flat abdomen. Her grandparents knew about the baby, but not about any of the true details of hers and Brad's marriage, or their separation. They still believed in Gwen's original version of why she married, and regretted as much as she did the coming divorce. But they had rallied around her, welcoming the news of her pregnancy and insisting that she stay with them after her graduation until the baby was born and she was able to seek work.

Naomi spoke from the doorway. 'The taxi's here.'

'Okay, thanks. Grandma, don't lift that suitcase, it's too heavy. I'll carry it.' Gwen reached for her tote bag and handbag, slung both over her shoulder, and hefted her large suitcase. 'All right, let's go.'

It was a subdued group that trooped out to the front porch. Even Julia's black mongrel puppy—her promised Christmas present—carried a sad expression. Amid hugs and kisses goodbye, Gwen promised to write, told a tearful Julia to be good, held tightly to her sister for a long moment, and showed a smiling face that fooled no one.

'Gwen, won't you please try again with Brad?' pleaded Naomi, clutching her hand.

'Naomi, please don't——'

'Just one more time, Gwen. For the baby?'

She wavered, and broke. 'All right,' she said in a hollow voice. 'One more time.'

'Promise?'

'Yes, I promise.'

The cab driver honked his horn impatiently. A final hug, a wave, and then Gwen was sitting chilled and alone in the back seat of the taxi, on her way to the airport and a promise she didn't know if she could bring herself to fulfil.

The terminal was crowded with travellers returning home from the Christmas holidays. Gwen checked her baggage, then politely excused her way through the throngs until she found an empty seat in which to wait for her flight to be called. People swirled about her—laughing, chattering, filling her ears with a cacophony of noise. Tucking her chin in the warm folds of her woollen scarf, she tried to shut out the rest of the world and the feeling of nausea the baby was causing. Her and Brad's baby.

Gwen almost doubled over in torment. When would her love stop hurting? She could tell herself over and over again that Brad didn't care, Brad didn't need, and

believe what she was saying, but her heart wouldn't let
go of what it had so fiercely and stubbornly fought for.
She was a wife needing her husband, longing for him,
and her baby would be a child needing and wanting its
father. And Brad would have been such a terrific one, if
only he'd loved as well as wanted. If he had, he'd be
with her now, discussing baby matters and no doubt
arguing good-naturedly with her about whose chore it
would be to change the nappies. They would agree on
split duties, and decide where to live and what to buy
and whether to breastfeed. He would cross-examine her
on what the doctor had said, and set up in his mind a
strict pre-natal diet for her to follow. He would be
nervous and proud, a little anxious about her, a lot
protective, and so very loving. So very, *very* loving. Oh,
God, why couldn't he be here? Their baby was a scary
responsibility, and she couldn't cope with it alone. She
needed Brad's help. She needed *him*.

'*What* an absolute *hunk* of a *man*!'

Gwen choked back a shaky laugh. The enthralled
statement reminded her of the first time she'd met Brad.
Nostalgia for that long-ago day filled her, and she
raised her head to compare her hunk with this other
one. A man in his early thirties was threading his way
through a group of children. One hand clutched a large,
silver-wrapped parcel to his chest. The other was curled
tightly around the metal handle of a wooden cat carrier.
He was undoubtedly the best-looking man Gwen had
ever seen. His face was a little thin, but his finely-
moulded features overcame this slight flaw. Electric
blue eyes were set beneath straight brows, the gentle
glow of warmth in them matching the tentative smile
that was faltering on his lips. He was taller than many
men around him, but moved with an uneven grace,
knowing where he was heading but not sure whether he
wanted to get there. Nervous, uncertain, vulnerable, he
looked to be the kind of man who seldom lost anything,
but when he did, and realised how much he missed it,
would search for the rest of his life until he found it, or
die trying.

The thought stirred the embers of a dying fire, and

Gwen looked blindly away from that familiar gaze. She wouldn't start hoping again, wouldn't put herself through a second visit to hell. *Please, Bradley,* she thought in fresh agony, *leave me alone. It's over between us.*

'Mrs Robilliard?'

She glanced up involuntarily, surprised by the formal mode of address. 'What?' Her voice cracked on the word.

'You *are* Gwen Robilliard, aren't you?'

'I . . . Yes.'

'I'm Brad Robilliard.' He looked down into her pale face, the present in one hand, the cat carrier in the other, and attracted instant attention from everyone within hearing distance with the quiet delivery of his next words. 'I don't know if you want to hear it, but I have a proposition to lay before you.'

'What kind—of proposition?' *Oh, hope, lie down and die.* Pain flickered in those shadowed eyes and Gwen knew that Brad, too, had fought to live through his suffering.

'If you will stay married to me and live with me for the rest of our lives, I will give you all the love and trust I took from you, and more.' He took a step forward—towards her, and their future—oblivious of the fascinated onlookers. 'I need you, Gwen. And love you. Will you come home with me?'

'Oh, Bradley,' she said softly, tremulously.

She rose to meet him halfway, going into his arms as he went into hers. Someone gently disengaged the cat carrier and gift from Brad's hands with a faintly humorous comment that elicited chuckles from the people around them.

'I love you, too, Bradley,' Gwen whispered against the male roughness of his jaw, tightening her arms about him. 'And I've missed you so much. I want to come home.'

Freed of his burdens, he shaped her slim body to the strong, loving length of his and took her mouth in a hard, hungry kiss that asked for forgiveness and promised forever, that gentled and clung, and finally drifted away with soft reluctance.

'Man, *that* was a *kiss*!' a teenaged boy declared enthusiastically.

Brad and Gwen broke apart, slightly embarrassed by their public reunion.

'Bradley, let's get *out* of here!' hissed Gwen with reddening cheeks.

'Trace has offered the use of his penthouse while he's out of town. There's a limo waiting outside. Come on.'

Brad gave a direction to the chauffeur and then pressed a button which slid a glass partition between the front and back seats. Strangely, Gwen found herself a little uncomfortable now that she was alone with him. Leaning forward, she peered into the cat carrier at her feet.

'It's awfully quiet in there. You'd think the kittens would be meowing at least.'

Brad rubbed the back of his neck ruefully. 'Er—I had them drugged a bit. They would have been terrified in the plane's cargo hold stone sober.'

'Oh, you poor kitties,' Gwen crooned, lifting them from the carrier to her lap. Max tried to stand up, staggered, and plonked back on to his stomach. 'They seem more drunk than drugged.'

'I swear, Gwen, I didn't force-feed them alcohol. The vet gave them a tiny fraction of a pill each, and presto, they were in dreamland, with nary a scratch to me, I might add.'

Bomber huddled miserably next to his brother, riding out the indignity of being plastered, his cross-eyed gaze fixed on Brad with total and utter loathing. Gwen had to laugh at his sorry condition.

'I don't think he's going to be very pleased with you for a while, Bradley.'

'I couldn't leave them behind, sweetheart. They're part of my life. As you are, and always will be. Gwen, I've been such a fool, a perfect bastard, and I'm so sorry for——'

She pressed quick, compassionate fingers to his mouth, silencing him. 'Darling, you don't have to tell me you're sorry. We've each made some major mistakes, and I think we both know how much they've hurt us. The most important thing is that we kept trying, even while thinking the worst of each other, and that's proved how much we regret what's happened. We'll go on now, and not dwell on the bad times. Okay, Bradley?'

He drew her into his arms, resting his cheek against the black softness of her hair. 'Okay, Gwen.' She didn't see the faint sparkle of tears in his eyes, and he blinked them quickly away. For so long he had walked alone, expecting always to travel in solitary darkness and never find the light that would bring him in from the cold. But it had found him, hovering brightly around his loneliness until it drove all the dark shadows away, never leaving him alone, always insisting on being noticed. And he, in his damned arrogance, had done his unconscious best to destroy it. But never again. Gwen, his bright light, his dream, would be loved and treasured until his final breath and beyond. She had given him her soul. Now, he would give her his.

Time was arrested, the world outside far away and forgotten. Lamplight danced over two supple golden bodies. Blond silk blended with black satin, temples becoming damp with perspiration as raw, mounting need blasted the room with fire. Passion crested, hung balanced, gripped to the core and then rippled through, leaving behind deep pleasure and lethargic contentment.

'When's it due?' murmured Brad, his hand gliding across the glowing sheen of Gwen's stomach.

'Early September.'

'Got a long way to go, then.'

She turned lazily until she was propped up against his chest. An exploring finger traced his lips. 'Our baby was conceived that first night, Bradley.' She caught his faint, secretive smile and realisation dawned. 'You wanted to make me pregnant right from the start, didn't you?' she asked in soft wonder.

'That's an understatement.' He swept her hair back over one creamy shoulder to better enable him to see her face. 'I felt that somehow it would make you truly and completely mine, that you wouldn't be able to leave me after the year was up.'

'Then why did you hang up when you heard that I was pregnant?'

'Because you'd been crying, and only then did I realise what a baby would do to your career plans. You'd worked so hard, and right from the beginning I'd known how important they were to you, yet I went ahead and——'

'Bradley, the only thing I want more than this baby is you,' Gwen interrupted. 'I was crying because I couldn't tell you I was pregnant. I didn't want you coming back to me only for the sake of our baby.'

He pulled her head down to his shoulder. 'Has it ever occurred to you, my lovely wife, that we don't talk enough?'

'The thought has more than once crossed my mind, yes,' she sighed. 'Bradley?'

'Hmmm?'

'What happened to us that day in December? We were so happy, and suddenly—there was all that hatred and coldness.'

'Leo happened to us. He told me you'd said you hated me during your talk the day you came to my office——'

'The——!' Gwen sat up, highly indignant. 'Bradley, I did not. The only time I said such a thing was at the apartment that Sunday night, and I certainly didn't *mean* it!'

'I know you didn't. That must have been what he was referring to. I was too stunned to think clearly. Then he told me how relieved you were that all your troubles were ended.'

'My troubles! I didn't *have* any troubles until he told me he was your uncle and that he'd warned you to be nice to me or he'd take back his loan.'

Brad groaned. 'He warned me, all right, and I told him not to push me that far. My God, if I'd known he'd said that to you I would have called him a blundering idiot and gone straight home to make sure you didn't put the wrong interpretation on it. Instead, I sat there listening to Leo tell me how you would never let love interfere with your career and how you would do anything to get money.'

'For my *family*! *Ooh*, I could—could *throw* something at him! How could he tell you that and not explain why?' Gwen flopped back against the pillows and clapped her hands over her eyes in groaning frustration. Leo! It had all been Leo! Well, most of it. Some godfather he was. She removed her hands and turned her head to look at him. 'Bradley, last April my parents and brother-in-law were killed in a car accident, and my sister and niece badly injured. I needed the money to pay massive hospital bills that were worrying my sister and grandparents sick. That's why I married you. No other reason.'

He gathered her close. 'Oh, honey, I'm sorry. No, I *will* say it this time. For your loss, and the grief I wasn't there to help you with. I lost my own parents when I was barely twelve, and I can still remember the gut-wrenching sense of bereavement. It must have been tough for you, and your snarling new husband didn't help any.'

'You helped, just by being there. It was enough to get me going again. But I should have told you, instead of being so paranoid that you'd use my financial dependency to make me toe the line.'

'Leo didn't tell me either, and he asked me not to tell you that he was my uncle. Leo,' added Brad reflectively, 'has a lot to answer for. I really don't think I chewed him out quite thoroughly enough.'

'You chewed him out?' asked Gwen in an approving tone.

'Not then. It was the next morning. I rousted him out of a board meeting and instructed him not to go near you, not to phone you, not even to think of you. I told him he was the worst matchmaker in history because he'd totally demolished the one match he'd made, and that if he poked his nose one iota of an inch into the shambles of our marriage neither you nor I would ever speak to him again. And I said if . . . *if* . . . we ever got back together again, he could count himself extremely fortunate to be invited to the real wedding we were going to have.'

'You're right, you didn.t chew him out enough.' The whole situation, now that it was over and no longer a threat to her marriage, was tickling Gwen's sense of humour now. Her shoulders shook with convulsed laughter. 'Leo and his matchmaking! I *wondered* why he kept phoning so often. And each time he did, I'd just had a fight with you, and filled his ear with all my woes.'

A responding laugh rumbled low in Brad's chest. 'And that night he visited us, I told him we fought every day.'

'Poor, *poor* man. We must have sounded like bitter enemies to him. No wonder he thought his match had failed!'

'The real irony is that he broke us up just when we'd given up fighting our marriage,' mused Brad.

'He must be feeling wretched. We really should put him out of his misery.'

'Yes, I suppose so.'

Brad and Gwen looked at each other and said on the same breath, 'But he will *not* be a godfather to our child!' They burst out laughing.

'I'll call him tomorrow,' said Brad, 'tell him we're staying married as a favour to him.'

'Do you think this has discouraged him as a marriage broker?'

'I don't know. Something he said makes me think he's got his eye on a wife for Trace next.'

'Oh-oh. We'd better warn your brother.'

'Nonsense. I struck it rich with the wife Leo found for me. Maybe Trace will have the same luck.'

'Mmm.' She settled comfortably in the cradle of his arms. 'I love you, Bradley.'

'I love you, Gwen.'

Immensely satisfied by this mutual exchange, they lay quietly, content to merely be together.

'Bradley?' Gwen said again, newly troubled. 'What

did your grandfather do to you?'

For a long moment she thought he wasn't going to answer, then expressionlessly, 'He paid my fiancée to have an abortion, and then to leave town. He didn't want me tied down so young, wanted me to focus all my attention on the company. It was summer, and I was working at the head office between university terms. I left, and never spoke to or saw my grandfather for thirteen years. Until last week.'

Gwen felt the sorrow that lingered, not for the breach between himself and his grandfather, but for the baby he would never know. She held Brad, and took into herself some of the hurt that he was finally sharing with her. 'Is that why you held yourself back from me, Bradley? Because you were afraid I'd betray you, too?'

'I might have had some doubts at first, but they didn't last. Gwen, I was ready to commit myself to you long before we first made love. But I thought your career was more important to you, so I assumed a wait-and-see attitude. I was absolutely floored when you said you loved me. I couldn't believe my luck, but told myself that you needed time to consider your career. Then, when I discovered you were pregnant, I thought I'd ruined everything. You were stuck with the baby I'd selfishly given you and probably hated me for what I'd done.' Brad brought her left hand to his lips, kissing the engagement and wedding rings which had been wrapped inside his large gift to her. 'But this morning, when I woke up, lightning struck. I believed, at last, that you loved me and wanted our baby. And I knew that our marriage would never keep you from reaching for the brightest star in the corporate field. I knew, beyond any shadow of a doubt, that we could have it all, you and I—if only I got to you in time.'

Gwen wound her fingers with his. When she could, she'd buy him a gold band and slip it on his wedding finger. Brad would like that, she knew. It breathed permanence and belonging. 'So the fault for your lack of commitment was mine all along,' she stated.

Brad heard the smile in her voice and responded in kind. 'Definitely your fault. All you had to do, sweet, was say three little words, and I would have been your slave for life. Now, I'm just your husband. Tough luck, eh?'

'I think I can live with that. Bradley, you said you saw your grandfather last week.'

'Yes. He'd bribed Pamela, and I felt that if he had half a chance, he'd try to bribe you if he learned our marriage was on the rocks. I knew it wouldn't work, but he could have seriously damaged our reconciliation if there was one. So I went to put him straight, threaten him if need be to forget he ever had a second grandson. It wasn't necessary.' Various emotions flitted across Brad's face as he remembered a confrontation which had never materialised. 'I found there was no feeling left for him. No hatred, no bitterness, and God knows there was never any love. He treated my sister Kristin as if she didn't exist and beat obedience into Trace and me when we were kids. None of us owe him anything, and as a result he has no one at his side in his old age. About all I do feel is indifference, and it's taken away all his power to hurt me.'

'Maybe some day he'll regret what he's done and—— '

'Maybe. We'll see.' Brad rolled over, pinning Gwen's body beneath his. 'Back to more important matters. Did I tell you I've made a list?'

She ran her finger down his nose. 'Of what? All your faults?'

'I have no faults,' he informed her. 'You've turned me into a paragon of virtue.'

'Then what does this list consist of?'

'Everything—names, nursery items, baby clothes. I want our child so much, Gwen. I want you.'

'In more ways than one,' she teased, shifting provocatively under him, wanting to erase the traces of sadness she could see in his eyes.

Brad's mouth came down in a slightly punishing kiss,

softened at the touch of her hands on his waist, lingered with a deep and thorough intimacy that promised to lead to further delights.

'Bradley, wait.' Gwen reached for the phone on the night table in Trace Robilliard's master suite and dragged it between them. 'I have to phone Naomi and my grandparents and let them in on the happy ending. After that,' she added graciously as she waited for an answer on the other end of the line, 'you may do with me what you will.'

'Thank you, I fully intend to.' He was already starting.

'Hello, Grandpa? It's Gwen ... I'm with my husband, Grandpa, and we're all coming for a visit tomorrow. Max and Bomber and Brad and me and the baby ...'

Some four and a half months later, Gwen graduated from university with first-class honours, and Brad was there to share in her accomplishment. And on the day after their first wedding anniversary, with her husband by her side, she gave birth to a raven-haired baby girl who immediately succeeded in wrapping her hapless father firmly around her tiny finger.

'She's going to be devastating when she grows up,' said Brad, cradling his daughter with infinite gentleness in his arms. 'Like someone else I know.' He looked up, a wicked glint in those blue, blue eyes. 'Can we make another one just like her?'

Gwen smiled at the picture her husband and child made against the background of flowers in the hospital room. She had reached for the brightest star—and found it in this man, this child. 'Perhaps a son next time. Michelle needs a male on whom she can practise her bossiness.'

Brad came over to settle the baby in her arms, watching intently as she freed a breast to let her hungry daughter nurse. Then, with simple love, he took a red rose from the huge bouquet on the night table, broke off the stem, and gently placed it in his wife's hand. 'For ever, Gwen,' he said huskily, meeting her eyes.

'Always and for ever.'

'Yes.' She touched rose and hand to his hard cheek. 'I love you, too, Bradley. So very, very much.'

His fingers curled around hers and, with hands clasped warmly together, they looked down at the nursing infant and watched their future grow.

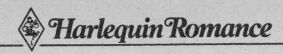 **Harlequin Romance**

Coming Next Month

Available in November wherever paperback books are sold, or through Harlequin Reader Service.

In the U.S.
P.O. Box 1397
Buffalo, N.Y.
14240-1397

In Canada
P.O. Box 2800, Postal Station A
5170 Yonge Street
Willowdale, Ontario M2N 6J3